Elaytay (Tay)'s Adventures in Space and Time

"We Came to Visit"

By

Lauresa Tomlinson

Young of Heart Publishing
P.O. Box 2274
McKinleyville, CA
95519

1998

Just a note… out beside each character's name you will find (their nick name). I hope this makes the story easier to read. After all, Alien/strange names are sometimes a little harder to pronounce.

As I lay here in this dark, damp vault of the King, my life is swirling before me.   I can see my youth as if it were yesterday.

And I find myself wondering what tomorrow will bring if I can find my way home again.

I hope they can find me in time to figure out the correct space-time configuration before the air gives out.

Elaytay (Tay)
The 7th of Satchur 2472

Table of Content

We Came To Visit

Chapter One
What a Bunch

Walking briskly, Master Enahsto (Master E) made his way down the winding path to the lake. Epsilon (Lonnie) was lying peacefully under a tree, watching the clouds drift lazily by.

"Epsilon (Lonnie)!" Master Enahsto (Master E)'s voice blasted loudly through his wandering thoughts.

Walking along the path to my first class at the Space Academy, I had noticed Master Enahsto (Master E) walking briskly towards the lake. Thinking it strange, I wondered who was teaching his class right now. Then I heard his booming voice bursting through the silence.

A few keptrons (minutes) later Epsilon (Lonnie) came running up the hill from the lake as if a fire was chasing him.

Waving my hands and yelling, I tried to slow him down. "Wait, Epsilon (Lonnie),"

He slowed down a little as I joined him. We ran together toward the classrooms as he related to me, between heavy breaths, what had happened.

Now Epsilon (Lonnie) was an old friend, and everyone that knew him, knew he would rather be napping under a tree somewhere than to be in a classroom. He had always been the joker of our little group. He was always trying to get out of something, especially if it meant work was involved. Epsilon (Lonnie) was a little shorter than me, with short blonde hair that would turn almost white in the sun. His large blue eyes and innocent looking features made it hard to believe that he was responsible for some of the pranks he had been caught doing.

"You know, I think that Master Enahsto (Master E) has a sintho that he is using to help teach class and give his test," he huffed.

"A sintho? You mean one of those android-type creatures that take on the personality and actions of their owner?" I ask.

"Yeah, yeah, one of those," he puffed. "I'm telling you, I just left him down by the lake and he is testing students inside at the same time. So you figure it out," still excited he took off running even faster for class.

It was already hot and it wasn't even noon yet. The purple skies of Cyterrious shined with an extra brilliance.

I had just received orders from the Space Missions Department of the United Planets Alliance and wanting to tell Master Enahsto (Master E) first, I walked faster.

I looked towards the lake then towards the science building and in the window of one of the classrooms I spotted Master Enahsto (Master E).

Walking into the science building, classes were just letting out, and there in the hallway, talking with another teacher was Master Enahsto (Master E).

He was one of the academy's best teachers. As always, he had on a long white flowing robe and a vestment of emerald green. His silver hair hung in shoulder-length waves on his long vestment. He had a slight limp to his right leg and was now getting ready to teach his next class at the Mission Academy.

"Master Enahsto (Master E), wait up!" I shouted.

He turned to see who was shouting at him. "Ah, Elaytay (Tay), what can I do for you?" he asked with a sparkle in his large, dark blue eyes. He always seemed to be happy and at peace with his life. As I came closer, the thought raced through my mind--would Master Enahsto (Master E) really use a sintho? Pushing the thought away...

"I just received the papers for my first space exploration and data tracking mission and I wanted to talk with you before I had to leave on my mission,"

"Well, I have a class right now, how about if we meet under the Boonak tree at noon?" he said looking toward his classroom.

"Okay, I'll see you then." I replied.

Turning he went into his classroom. I ran down the hall and got through the classroom door just as the bell sounded. Hurrying to my seat, I managed to sit down before the teacher turned around.

This class always seemed to go by very fast. I loved to study the behaviors and health of the different races and life forms we had discovered. Our people, as well as others from the Alliance, had been tracking the progress of life and collecting data from other planets for a long time. My next class was the study of plants, their uses and what each race used them for. Where these plant used for food or medicine, or just for shelter and recreation. In this class, I was required to learn the major planets, the plant life, the regions in which they grew, and their purposes and usage.

Everyone that was assigned to exploring teams was also required to learn basic medical training and survival techniques.

Snatching up my books I headed for the Boonak tree. I got there early so I could take a closer look at my mission orders before Master Enahsto (Master E) arrived.

I've always loved the Boonak tree. It was always cool in its shade, even on the hottest sestrons (days). When I was younger, all of the kids from my area would have club meetings under its branches because of the way it grew. It was the only type of tree that had anywhere from three trunks to as many as eight at the same time, and all of its major branches grew together.

When I received my papers to travel, I was also given the names of the other team members and the solar systems we were to explore and help. Sometimes missions were just to explore the worlds and take data on the different types of creatures, plants, races, waters, soils and air. That way we could better track the progress of each planet we discovered.

Taking a look at the team members list for my mission, I found that Elatron (Tron) was going to be the captain. It was going to be hard for me to call Elatron (Tron), "Captain". We had grown up in the same area and everyone had called him Tron, and now, I was going to have to call him "Captain!" I had never thought of him as a Captain, but we had always chosen him to lead our group when we went exploring. We knew he could be very stern when times called for it and playful at other times, but always fair. He was always big for his age, and knew what he wanted. Even then he stood two to three lanfas (inches) taller than most, with dark collar-length hair, dark, almost black eyes, and was always well groomed.

Seeing the next member's name, made my heart sink, it was Epsilon (Lonnie). He was to be our navigator. Our nickname for him was "Oops" because of the blunders he had caused as a teenager. I didn't think he had grown any since he was 14 sectos (years) old. He was still short and wastes time goofing off instead of studying. I would often see him sleeping under a tree near the lake instead of going to class. Having Epsilon (Lonnie) as our navigator on this trip, gave me a bad feeling.

"Elaytay (Tay)," Master Enahsto (Master E)'s voice burst through the quiet and startled me. I jumped and he laughed, "I didn't think I had been that quiet! And I didn't think that a young woman of your training would be so jumpy."

"I was looking over my travel orders and sestron (day) dreaming."

"About what, may I ask?" he asked softly.

Pointing to my list, "Well, I just noticed Epsilon (Lonnie) is going to be our navigator, and as an elder, you must remember as well as I do, how he used to get all of us kids into trouble,"

He patted me gently on the back. "Sometimes people change. Give him another chance."

Protesting I tried to explain, "But I can remember a time when he got us all lost in the Caves of Omalon, and if it weren't for the extraordinary senses of our pet nanastoo (small monkey type animal) we would have died there."

"He has had many classes of training now and has proven himself on other short missions. He will do a good job," Master Enahsto (Master E) encouraged.

"I just want to make it back in one piece. I still have my doubts," I said feeling worried.

"Let's see who else you have on your team," he said, as he changed the subject, and looked over my shoulder at the list.

Looking at the list again I saw Elazephron (Laz) as engineer and that made me smile.

"Elazephron (Laz) is going to be our engineer. I like him. When we were younger we called him "Zephee" and I had a crush on him." I said, feeling shy.

"And still do I suspect?" he questioned, raising one eyebrow.

Feeling suddenly shy, "Well, yes, I guess I do, sort of," I answered while shuffling one foot.

"Does he know that? Does he know that you had, and still have a crush on him?" Master Enahsto (Master E) prodded.

"I don't think so. Grams said it may get in the way of our studies, so I've just kept it to myself," I answered looking down at the ground.

"Why do you think you like him so much?" he asked with a grin.

"He's always been a kind and considerate person. He has gone out of his way to help others and me when we needed it. He's tall, strong, and smart with the deepest brownest eyes of anyone I've ever met. And besides when our eyes meet, I feel like I'm going to melt." Then realizing what I had just said, I started laughing with embarrassment as I gathered my thoughts "Now wait just a keptron (minute). I feel like I'm under the lagascope (microscope). I came to talk to you about the mission, not about me." I playfully protested.

Chapter Two
Getting to Know

"Well, who is the medical officer?" Master Enahsto (Master E) inquired with a small grin, looking toward the list.

"Ezethron (Zeth) is. Well that sounds about right. He was always testing the hair of his pet tapnah or something, looking for some type of insect or new cell structure." I said.

Ezethron (Zeth)'s tapnah was a little different than most. It had rusty colored fur with splotches instead of being all black, but it still had the large green eyes, a yellow nose, long pointed ears and sort of bear-shaped face, and was still the size of a medium dog with a long fluffed tail.

He Looked thoughtfully into space, then answered "Yes! He was very busy as a child, collecting data on different species. It seemed that every time I saw him he was carrying a different book on science research and data,"

"He's in my study class for plant life of other worlds," I informed Master Enahsto (Master E).

"Well, it sounds like you're on a good team for your first mission. It seems that the overseers looked over the teams pretty well now...not like when I was young," he said thoughtfully, as if he was thinking back.

"Someone said that was how you got your limp...I mean, uh, on an exploration," I said, stumbling for the right words.

"Yes," he paused to put his hand on his leg. "It seems long ago in another life time, but I was just about your age and always in a hurry. We had just landed. I was assigned to gather samples of soil and water. I got off the ship on the second planet in the third solar system and went running to a nearby stream. Oh, I forgot, you would know it as Obatron 2 or 2/3SS." said Master Enahsto (Master E) thoughtfully.

"Oh…yes, go on," I encouraged him to continue.

"Let me tell you something before I go on with my story. It is very important to study the plants and animals of each planet before you leave on these missions to gather more data. I learned that important lesson the hard way. I didn't do any studying because, at the time, I thought it was a waste of time, sort of like Epsilon (Lonnie)." he chuckled.

"Well, as I started to tell you, I took off for the stream in a hurry, but little did I know that the plants on this planet trapped their prey. I assume, you have read about the Pujno plant on Panopia, the one that can move as quickly as some of the animals there. Those plants have survived the ages by wrapping around passing animals and dissolving them with an acid they make. Well, I almost became dinner. It ended up with a fight between a zatoth (saber-tooth tiger type) beast and this vine-type plant that had me trapped. It seems they both wanted to have me for dinner. The plants on this planet were like those on Panopia. And if it weren't for Esnay (Naus), one of my team members, I would have been eaten that sestron (day). Instead, I ended up with an injured leg. I got the limp because of infection that set in before we could get back to the star base." he continued.

"Well, you needn't worry about me," I explained. "I've been studying about the planets we will be traveling to. For instance, on the first planet we are to visit, Palids, there are several creatures and races of interest. The one race has dark green skin, yellow hair, large ears and bright blue eyes. They can see in the dark and they like meeting new races and are a very friendly people. Our scientists have been teaching them about the plants on other parts of their planet and their healing properties. This race likes farming but don't care for science too much." I said.

"Oh!" I said catching my breath, "I wish you could see this one creature they have on this other planet, Gramps was telling me about it. I've only seen holographic pictures of it. It's about the size of our oomeno (small pony type animal), 5 lifnas (feet) tall. It has bright orange fur on its body and almost florescent yellow feathers on its head. It has an almost flat face with big green eyes and a long prehensile tail. I wish I had one for a pet. They are very smart, and learn quickly. But if they are frightened, they can put out an odor that would turn the nose of a canapell (an anteater type animal). They are called Sapindos."

"What about the chance of cloning one by bringing back DNA samples?" Master Enahsto (Master E) questions with a chuckle.

"I was thinking about that earlier. I thought about maybe, asking Ezethron (Zeth) to see if he could get permission from the Counsel to clone some of the creatures from the DNA we gather. I know that in the past some creatures were okay to bring back as long as they were a certain size or smaller and wouldn't harm people," I said, hinting at the idea.

"I would love to see a public viewing place for animals of other planets. We used to have a lot of animals before our race went through its temper tantrums and killed over half of the population, most of the plants and polluted the water, air and soil. Most all of the animals became extinct due to pollution and our misuse of nature. We are really lucky that as many of our plants, animals and races survived that did. In our early sectos (years), our own planet was a very violent place to live. Our planet has gone through a lot of changes, and so did the people before we all learned to live together," he explained.

"I remember the stories that Gramps told me when I was younger about times of war, bombs, explosions, death and destruction. But, I always thought they were just stories. I never thought they were true," I said, thinking about all of the other things Gramps had told me.

I found myself wondering if they were all true. He had spoken of a few other planets that became void of life because of humankind's foolishness and ego trips, always seeking power. "He always told me to pray that humankind would soon learn where the real power comes from and would stop their abuse of creation." I continued.

"Not to change the subject, but how are you doing with the languages of the planets you will be going to?" Master Enahsto (Master E) asked slightly tilting his head.

"Well, Grams has been to the second planet we will be visiting and she knows some of the main languages there. She has taught me from an early age most of them because she liked the way they sounded. I know the language of, 'The People of the Sun, The People of the Wind and The People of the Singing Words'. Grams always said that 'The People of The Singing Words', sound as if they singing when they talk. But if you sing the wrong note in the wrong place, you can accidentally say something other than what you want to say. That language sounds really strange sometimes. Then there are two more races, I can't remember what Grams called them, but they cut off their words very quickly and one even makes a clicking sound when they speak. On that planet there are some really strange languages. Oh but, I'll have my side translator with me just in case." I explained.

"I'm glad to hear that you're learning so much," Master Enahsto (Master E) said, looking at his timelink. "Oh! I have to go, I have another class to teach." waving as he hurried off.

'He's still in a hurry', I remember thinking to myself with a Chuckle.

Chapter Three
Cloning

I gathered up my books and headed down the path towards Grams and Gramps' house. They didn't live too far from the Mission Academy. I had lived with them ever since Mom and Dad turned up missing on their last mission seven sectos (years) ago. Mom and Dad often told me that Grams and Gramps were a great source of information.

As I rounded the corner I could see Gramps working in his garden. He looked up from his work as I got closer to him.

Greeting me, Gramps gave me a big hug, "How's my best granddaughter doing this fine sestron (day)?"

"Your only granddaughter is doing really good this sestron (day), thank you," I said giggling.

"Well what question or riddle do you have for me this sestron (day)?" he inquired.

And before I could say anything, he put his arm around me and said in a low voice so no one else could hear, "Have you told Elazephron (Laz) how you feel about him yet?"

"Gramps, sometimes I think you are trying to be a match maker," I said feeling myself beginning to smile.

"Well, I think you two would make a good couple. I know Grams thinks differently. But she has always been the kind that said 'You can't afford to take chances while you are in the Mission's service.' But I like him, so what's new?"

Holding up my papers, "I hurried home to tell you, I received my travel papers a few decons (hours) ago."

"Well, I guess this calls for a party! Grams! Grams!" he yelled while taking my papers.

"Yes, dear, what do you need?" she asked as she came to the door wiping her hands with her apron.

"Look what I have in my hand," Gramps said hurrying toward the house waving my travel papers in the air.

"Elaytay (Tay), my dear, I didn't see you there behind your grandfather. I'm glad your home, I baked a new kind of cookies this sestron (day). Come on in my loves," she said greeting me with a kiss. Then turning to Gramps with a smile, "Now let me see what it is that you're waving around."

"Look at whose name is at the top of the paper!" he said waving the paper again excitedly.

I remember thinking that Gramps was more excited than me if that was possible.

"Well, stop waving them around and give them here." Grams said laughing as she reached for them.

"Oh!" she said getting a look at the papers then giving me a big smile, "Your first mission, I'm so thrilled for you. I can remember my first mission like as if it were sacytron (yesterday)."

"Look who the team members are," Gramps said poking the papers, while almost jumping up and down.

"Oh, well I'll be. It looks like most of the ol' gang is going on this mission together. Now is that luck or what?" she said smiling "That's nice." she added.

"Remember Gramps, the orange creature you told me stories about a long time ago? Well, I'm going to the planet where they live and then, the second one is," I said turning to Grams, "the planet where the people speak in the languages you've been teaching me. Isn't that great? I'm so excited!" I informed them.

Gramps leaned over and looked closely at me. "What are you cooking up in that head of yours now?" he questions, with a slight grin.

"Well, I thought that just maybe we (Ezethron (Zeth) & I) could get the council to let us bring back some DNA samples to clone. That way we would have a few more animals on this planet again. I mean we have so very few left, you know?" I said with a grin.

"Yes, I agree that it would be nice to have creatures running about again, but trying to get the council to go along with the idea won't be easy," Gramps said jumping into the conversation.

"Grams, can I use the telelink? I need to meet with Ezethron (Zeth)," I said, rubbing my hands together.

"Sure, honey, go ahead," she said with a nod.

As I went into the living room to get in touch with Ezethron (Zeth) I could hear Gramps talking to Grams. "You know darling, I think if anyone can get the council to give the okay, I think it will be our talented granddaughter and Ezethron (Zeth). They are both smooth talkers."

"You know, dear, I think you may be right. It would be nice to see lots of different animals on this planet again. I really miss the beautiful fowl and their lovely songs on Okanis 3." Grams said slowly as if to be remembering the beauty of that planet.

I was almost laughing as I came back into the room.

"Okay, Miss Cheshire cat, what's the word?" Gramps ask.

"Well, I told Ezethron (Zeth) about my idea and he loves it. It seems that the thought had passed through his mind as well. In fact he has already talked to the scheduler and got an appointment. He said we can get the council's attention on the idea by showing them the connection to scientific research. He seems to have high hopes for our project," I answered almost bouncing with happiness.

"What time do you have to meet with him?" asked Grams.

"Right around 15:35," I said, looking down at my timelink.

"Oh No! If I don't hurry I'll be late!" I gathered up two more of Grams' cookies, and took another sip of my tea, before running out the door. "I'll call you later to let you know how it went," I shouted as I waved goodbye while running down the front steps.

Running towards our meeting place, my mind raced through all of the different creatures I had been reading about. Some of the holographics were very exciting while others gave me a fearful feeling. But the idea of a public viewing area made from cloned animals was a wonderful idea. Up ahead I could see Ezethron (Zeth) standing with his arms folded and tapping his left foot.   "So, what is your excuse?" he asked with a slight smile.

"How late am I?" I asked almost out of breath. I breathed a little easier once I realized he was teasing.

"Just in time, in fact we have about ten keptrons (minutes) before we meet with the Council of Elders," he explained.

"Just for the sake of knowledge, is Master Enahsto (Master E) still on the Council of Elders?" I asked.

"Yes, I believe he is. Why do you ask?" he asked.

"Because if he is? Then we will have at least one vote for our cause. He is the one that reminded me of the idea of cloning the DNA samples we bring back," I said.

"Well, it's time to go put our idea before the council and see what they say," he said gathering up the data he had brought.

Walking into the council chamber, I realized how nervous I was. The Council of Elders had a lot of power over our lives and our space missions. They were the ones to make the laws, rules and regulations for our planet. Ezethron (Zeth) did most of the talking and Master Enahsto (Master E) asked just the right questions to put our idea in a favorable light with the council. Then we went to a waiting room and waited. It seemed like forever before we finally got the go ahead.

So now when we left on our mission, we were to take extra DNA samples containers to carry back the samples. We were also told to get DNA from both a male and female of each species.

Chapter Four
Planet Palids

The next few pestrons (weeks) passed quickly for me.

Before I realized it, it was time to get ready for the mission. I stayed up late to pack everything I knew I would need and made sure I had everything on the mission's list. One of the main things I had to remember was that my personal inventory limit was only 25 kepos (pounds).

The sectron (day) of our departure finally arrived. While standing at attention on the ship's ramp, I remember looking around as did the rest of our crew, to see who had come to see us off. Each of the council members gave a short speech to the crowd before we entered the ship.

We finally got the okay from the space port to enter the ship. We strapped in and started the take-off procedures. We were off the planet in a matter of keptrons (minutes).

On one memorable sestron (day), after three mistrons (months) of travel, I remember waking up for my sectronly (daily) duties, knowing that we were to land soon and take care of our first mission. I grabbed a bite to eat and went to work organizing my notes and data about the planet we were beginning to orbit. I was the communications officer aboard the Scout Ship Tauntus. One of my other duties was to help with the science data we were to retrieve. We had a crew of five, and were just getting ready to land on the fourth orb in the third solar system, Palids.

"Okay, people, you know your duties and the procedures." Captain Elatron (Tron) said sternly. "Elaytay (Tay), report," he continued.

"Landing markers located, and the okay for landing has been received. Diplomat Mastinar (Mast) and party are waiting our arrival, Sir!" I answered.

"Landing coordinates are noted and procedures taken, Sir!" Epsilon (Lonnie) reported.

"Landing has the green light, Captain, Sir!" reported Elazephron (Laz).

"Everything in the lab is secured for landing, Sir!" Ezethron (Zeth) said with a smile.

"Elaytay (Tay), open comlink," instructed Captain Elatron (Tron).

"Open, Sir. Diplomat Mastinar (Mast) on-line," I reported.

"Greetings, Diplomat Mastinar (Mast), this is Captain Elatron (Tron) of the Scout Ship Tauntus. We are landing now and will greet your party in three of your keptrons (minutes), Captain Elatron (Tron) out."

"I hope we get the okay to go into the countryside. I want a chance to see a zoobano up close," said Elazephron (Laz).

"A zoo--what?" asked Ezethron (Zeth).

"Yeah, it's sort of a cross between a pegacorn and a dragalon (the flying dragon type animal on Okanis 3)," Elazephron (Laz) tried explaining.

"A what and what?" Epsilon (Lonnie) questioned, jumping in on the conversation as he elbowed Ezethron (Zeth) and grinned.

I remember just sitting quietly and waited to hear the description Elazephron (Laz) was going to come up with. I looked around at the crew and they were listening very closely, too. Then I looked over and grinned at Captain Elatron (Tron).

"Well, a zoobano is an animal that has medium sized wings of red, yellow and orange feathers. It has a long neck, its chest back and tail have green scales. On its forehead is a golden horn and it has short legs in back with longer legs in front. Its stomach is covered in light blue fur with ginger brown spots, looks sort of like the cloth of an old jacket. The face almost looks like a fantasy creature in the reading material of Okanis 3. It has very large black eyes, round cheeks and a dragalon type snout." Elazephron (Laz) tried explaining. "You'll just have to see one before you'll know what I'm talking about," he continued as he saw the strange looks on our faces.

"I'm not sure how much sight-seeing we will be allowed to do on this mission. We have to take care of our assignments first," Captain Elatron (Tron) interrupted.

The doors opened, the ramp of our ship was lowered and we stepped out. We were greeted by Diplomat Mastinar (Mast) and his party Nostah (Nas) and Paneto (Pan).

Mastinar greeted our captain and nodded at the rest of us as we were introduced.

"I'm glad you could come at this time. We have been having problems with the over-population of a foul called Marpolan," he said.

I guess we all looked puzzled at him because he went on to describe the bird. "This bird has a wing span of six lifnas (feet). It has a bright blue body with a green head, yellow beak, and red ring around its neck and brilliant rainbow plumage springing from the top of its head, tail and wing tips. Some of our villages are really low on food at this point because this bird is raiding their gardens and fields. There are too many of these birds on this planet now. We need your help with this problem." he continued, as he handed us a holographic picture of a Marpolan.

We all stood still and studied the picture for a few keptrons (minutes).

"It's beautiful." I finally said looking at Captain Elatron (Tron).

Captain Elatron (Tron) looked over at Ezethron (Zeth) and me. We nodded. "Yes, I think we may be able to help with this problem," he said as he looked back at Diplomat Mastinar (Mast).

"Nostah (Nas) and Paneto (Pan) will help you with your needs," Diplomat Mastinar (Mast) said as he gestured with his hand toward them.

Nostah (Nas) was about my age, 16, with long blonde hair, light blue eyes, light skin and very personable. She was dressed in a light pink form-fitting jump suit with pale purple soft mid-thigh boots. She was small framed and looked to weigh about 118 kepos (pounds). She greeted us with a warm smile and a nod of her head. Paneto (Pan), on the other hand, was of medium build, well proportioned, of medium height, with dark shoulder-length hair and large dark eyes. He was dressed in a short tunic of light green and soft skinned mid-calf boots for easy movement. He greeted us with a large smile and a bow.

Then reaching out their hands in an open-armed gesture they spoke in unison. "Come. We will show you around. First we will show you our science areas and labs," they said, urging us to follow them.

Captain Elatron (Tron) had gone with Diplomat Mastinar (Mast).

Following Nostah (Nas) and Paneto (Pan) we walked into what I thought, was just a large building from the outside appearance. Once inside it was not at all what I expected. There were living areas for all different types of animals complete with the environment they normally lived in. But I didn't see any walls or divisions between the different animals. There were a lot of plants, streams, meadows, small lakes and waterfalls. I could even see the outside sky.

"What keeps the animals from killing each other and flying away?" I asked looking at Nostah (Nas).

"We have set up an invisible force field around each group. And if the power source should fail, walls will spring up out of the ground level and a net covers the top," she explained, with a smile. "We have tried to make sure that we have at least two pairs of each different type of creature on our planet in our PAFOW," she added.

"PAFOW?" I questioned.

"Yes, a place of safety for our plants and animal life. In case something happens where we lose most of the plants and animal life we know, we will have at least a couple of pairs of each species to start over," she explained.

"Yes, that is a good idea. We don't have any PAFOW yet, but we have the okay now to gather DNA samples of plants and animals to help get a PAFOW started when we get back home," I said.

"Come," said Paneto (Pan), with his arm stretched out towards another area. Following him he led us into a large room with lab tables and holding areas for animals. There were all sorts of instruments and lab equipment to use. This place was set up like a dream lab; there would be no excuse for not getting the research done that we had been assigned to do.

Ezethron (Zeth) stood there for a micron (second) with large eyes and his mouth slightly open. Finding his voice he said, "You mean this is where we will be working on the problem your planet is having?"

"Yes, and if you need anything else just let us know," replied Paneto (Pan).

Ezethron (Zeth) was still a little overwhelmed but managed a reply. "Sure, but it looks like everything is right here. Thank you."

Chapter Five
What an Idea

Paneto (Pan) bowed and left with Elazephron (Laz), saying something about engineering.

"Come. I will show you your sleeping chambers," motioned Nostah (Nas).

So we both followed Nostah (Nas) down the hallway with Epsilon (Lonnie) not far behind. Then she motioned to Ezethron (Zeth) that the first room was his. As he entered, he stuck his head out the door and shouted to me, "I will meet you in the lab in a decon (hour), okay?"

"Sure," I said, "see you later."

Then Epsilon (Lonnie) and I followed Nostah (Nas) down the hall a little farther and she showed me my room. As she took Epsilon (Lonnie) to his room, I walked into mine and was taken by surprise. The rooms were large and there was a small waterfall flowing from a mountain scene on one wall, with plants and rock for the water to flow over and around. The stream from the waterfall went half way out into the center of the room and then went under the floor. There were a lot of plants, beautiful furniture and wonderful wall scenes. In the bathing room was what almost looked like a small swimming pool. Then I looked up. There was no roof! The door buzzed and Nostah (Nas) walked in.

"Any questions yet?" Nostah (Nas) asked with a smile.

"Yes, what if it rains?" I asked pointing at the ceiling.

"Oh, not to worry, there is a force shield over the roof area so you can see out but nothing can get in," she explained with a smile. "You may want to relax for a while before going to work. And the next meal will be served in about four of your decons (hours). I will see you later," she said with a bow before leaving the room.

I remember being too excited to relax, so I looked around my room some more. I found a desk-like work area complete with a compulink and comlink that slid out of the wall when my fingers brushed over a small button on a shelf next to some books I had been looking at. I knew my way around most compulinks and had no trouble accessing this one. I found the history of the planet, brief outlines of their wars, and solutions to problems they had in the past. Also there is a list of plants and animals with their descriptions, that had been lost before the PAFOWs were set up. I got lost in the studies and before I knew it Ezethron (Zeth) was at my door. I greeted him, grabbed his hand and brought him into my room.

"Do you believe these rooms?" Ezethron (Zeth) said sounding amazed.

"Aren't they great? I was just accessing their compulink and found all kinds of great information. Want to see?" I asked pointing at the console.

"Not now. We have other things to do." he said tilting his head towards the door.

"Where is Epsilon (Lonnie)?" I asked.

"He's in the room on the other side of yours. I tried to get him to come to the lab to help, but he gave me this song and dance about how tired he was and that he was going to lie down for a while first," Ezethron (Zeth) replied.

"I hope he doesn't cause any trouble while we are here." I said as we left my room and walked to the lab.

Once in the lab we went straight to work on the problem at hand. After a few experiments we finally came up with a workable solution. We had about a decon (hour) before it was time for their next meal.

Nostah (Nas) came into the room about that time. "How are you doing on the problem?"

"I think we may have found a solution," said Ezethron (Zeth).

"I came to ask if you would like to see our Creation Domes?" asked Nostah (Nas).

We both looked puzzled at each other and then back at her. "A what dome?" I asked.

"We call them our Creation Domes. Really, they are special rooms that are used to teach our children about science, history and possible futures. We can program their compulink with the possibilities for either future problems or past happenings, and then the children walk into the chamber and solve the problems and learn by experiential interaction," she explained.

"I would love to see the Creation Domes," I said looking at Ezethron (Zeth).

"Yes, me too," he piped up.

So off we went down the hallway to a small room where we got into a small cylinder-type car on a rail in a clear tube. We went shooting through a tunnel with rows of intermittent lights, and after what seemed only a few microns (seconds) we stopped and got out, into another small room. Nostah (Nas) told us that we were on the other side of their planet. While I was there, I observed completely different types of plants and animals than on the other side of the planet. We both stopped and looked at Nostah (Nas) for an explanation.

Nostah (Nas) looked back over her shoulder at us and almost started to laugh. "Confused yet?" she asked with a giggle.

"Yes, you may say so," I said almost laughing. Her giggle was contagious. Ezethron (Zeth) and I both started laughing.

"Well, come on and I will show you even more things on our planet and when we get to the Creation Domes, you won't be confused anymore," she said motioning for us to hurry up. "This is our space observatory where we can all see how our planet works with all of the others we now know about. We can also study the other solar systems that we have information on." We walked past a very large domed building. "And these are our engineering labs, where our young students work on their own ship designs, with guidance, of course. All experiments, inventions and designs are recorded for their future use." Pointing to another building she added, "In that building over there our youngsters are learning the cloning processes of plants and animals. In fact, that area may be of interest to both of you." she said looking back at us with a smile. "But first things first, I will take you on a tour of our planet and the Creation Domes are the quickest way. We have found that the Creation Domes are the best way to experience the most in life without using much of our natural resources. We can program the Creation Domes to give us certain experiences. So, instead of wasting time, using fuel and wasting natural resources to make special equipment to gain an experience, we can just program the dome. The experiences are just as real as if you were there, because the mind thinks it is real and so the bones do break and you do get wounds, the same as if you really had the experience, unless you are very strong minded. Well, we are here."

I looked up as we entered this very large dome. Once inside I could see that it was divided into different areas with almost mirror-like walls. There seemed to be a specula difference; it seemed larger inside than it did outside.

"Why," I started to ask, and was interrupted.

"Why does it seem larger inside than it does outside?" Nostah (Nas) asked the question for me.

"Yes," I said, waiting for a long answer.

"That is an easy answer. When you stepped into this building you stepped into the next dimension where time and space is only relevant to the program that is being run at the time. That is why a person could come here and gain the experience they want or need with no loss of time or energy. In the Creation Domes, time doesn't exist the way we know it outside. We can stay in here for, let's say, three decons (hours) and when we walk back out those doors we would be in the same time and space as when we walked in. But the experiences will remain with you," she explained.

"Wow. Now that's a captivating thought, experiences without loss of time. I like that. Can a lab be set up in here?" asked Ezethron (Zeth).

Nostah (Nas) nodded, and led us into one of the Creation Domes' creative areas.

"Now what would you like to experience?" she asked.

While my mind was racing every which way with ideas, Ezethron (Zeth) spoke up. "How about a cloning experiment?"

"Why does your mind only run on one thing. Cloning!" I asked, sort of upset.

"Yes, that will be no problem," Nostah (Nas) answered Ezethron (Zeth)'s question. Then turning to me, she said, "Remember. In here, we are the controllers of time and not the other way around. So just relax and have fun. There is time for everyone."

That was sort of a relief. I didn't have to worry about having time run out because I owned all the time in all of creation. "I like the idea of not having to hurry in order to finish a project," I said with a smile.

"A lot of our students come here to run experiments that would normally take a lot of time. In here, you can speed up or slow time down," Nostah (Nas) said giving us even more ideas to play with.

When we came to a stopping point, we left the Creation Domes and went back to the lab. We had just finished logging in the data

from our experiments we had run in the
Creation Dome when the call came saying it
was time for the next meal.

Chapter Six
Epsilon (Lonnie) and the Zoobano

When we walked into the room where everyone had gathered for the meal, we were surprised again. There were long, well decorated tables with so many different types of dishes on them, that if you ate just a few bites from each dish it would take at least four decons (hours) just to sample half of them.

Nostah (Nas) told us that their planet was used to playing host to at least five different planets at one time. That was why there were so many different types of foods being offered at the meals. She walked in with us and pointed to our group.

"Did you know they have what they call Creation Domes?" I said nudging Elazephron (Laz) as I sat down next to him. "And they…"

"Yes, I know, without the loss of time," Elazephron (Laz) interrupted me. "I was there earlier this sestron (day) running a new engine I've been working on for the last three sectos (years). I had a chance to prove that it works. I'm going to make some changes to our engine before we leave this planet. I'm calling it my, Crystaline Magnetic Flux Drive with a Static Electro Generator."

"Okay mister smarty pants with the big word. Just what does all that mean?" piped up Epsilon (Lonnie) as he swallowed hard.

"Well, Epsilon (Lonnie), it means we will soon be able to travel faster," Elazephron (Laz) said.

"You would know more if you did something with your time beside waste it," I scolded.

"I can't help it if I need more sleep than most," he interjected.

"You can't find a medical person on any planet that would agree with you needing all the sleep you manage to get," I said, trying to imply laziness.

"All right! Enough you two," interrupted Captain Elatron (Tron). "Epsilon (Lonnie), you are going to have to get with the program a little better than you have," he said in a reprimanding tone.

"Yes, Sir," Epsilon (Lonnie) said bowing his head.

Captain Elatron (Tron) looked over at me. "So what have you two been up to this sestron (day)?"

"Well, I think we have found a solution to the bird problem and we were able to prove a few of our own theories," I said proudly.

"We also did some experiments on cloning and the growth processes of different species that we may be able to take home with us via DNA samples," Ezethron (Zeth) added.

"Good, I'm glad to see most of the team taking advantage of the equipment we are given to use here on this planet," said Captain Elatron (Tron) while looking at Epsilon (Lonnie), who was still shoveling in food like he wouldn't eat again for sectos (years).

When we were through with our meal we were given time for our own projects and studies; "off-time" as most of us called it.

The next morning we were up early and at our experiments again to see if we had overlooked anything before we really put our ideas into reality.

Meanwhile, Epsilon (Lonnie) had talked someone into taking him where there were live Zoobanos. It would have been bad enough if he had decided to use the Creation Domes for his visit or see them in a PAFOW, but, no, he had to go see the real thing, in the wild. When word reached us as to where Epsilon (Lonnie) had gone, our whole team jumped into an antigravity shuttle and took off to where he was. Epsilon (Lonnie) had always been one to throw caution to the wind. When he had something set in his head, he would go all out to do it no matter what. And this time seemed to be one of his "no matter what" times.

We arrived just in time to see him do battle with this great creature. It was trying to fly, but hopping was the best it could do because of how small its wings were in proportion to its body. It kept hopping towards Epsilon (Lonnie) and breathing puffs of hot air on him. He had a shield and a sword held up in front of him but in comparison with the size of the zoobano it was no contest. The zoobano finally got tired of playing and with one large swoop he hit Epsilon (Lonnie) so hard that he rolled and bounced twice. Needless to say, Epsilon (Lonnie) stayed down. He was knocked out cold.

The guides that brought Epsilon (Lonnie) to fight the zoobano ran off the beast with a couple of blasts of their zap guns.

"Zoobanos like to play fight, but they won't start a fight. But if someone starts a fight they will oblige them," the guides explained.

We gathered up Epsilon (Lonnie) and took him back to the medical area of the planet. After the medical exams, the doctors sent word to us by an intern. "He will be fine. He had a few broken ribs and had the wind knocked out of him but he is fine," the intern reported to Elazephron (Laz) and me.

We all agreed that Epsilon (Lonnie)'s being okay was good news. I couldn't help but to hope that he had learned something from all of this.

Next morning came early. Ezethron (Zeth) and I were ready for field experiments on the pesky birds. But first we had to explain to Diplomat Mastinar (Mast) what experiment we had proven to be effective. Captain Elatron (Tron) went with us to see Diplomat Mastinar (Mast).

"Diplomat Mastinar (Mast)," Captain Elatron (Tron) said as we bowed and proceeded to talk in a low voice.

"Ezethron (Zeth) and Elaytay (Tay)," Diplomat Mastinar (Mast) replied in acknowledgment. We bowed again in respect to him.

"Your captain has told me that if anyone could find a solution to our problem that you two can," Diplomat Mastinar (Mast) said looking at Ezethron (Zeth) and me. "So tell me, what do you have?"

"We have been working in your planet's Creation Domes on the bird problem

and have come up with a two-part solution,"
I explained.

"Oh, good, Go on," he said.

Ezethron (Zeth) started to explain.
"Well what we have found by studying this
particular fowl is that they mate twice each
secto (year) and each pair have an average of
two chicks each time. What we propose is, to
put up force fields over the crops so that the
birds can't get to them, and at the same time,
put up troughs of grain soaked in spency
solution to control the birth rate. I would
estimate that the spiked grain would only
have to be used for maybe one of your sectos
(years). The spency that will stay in their
systems for two sectos (years) after the last
feeding, so make sure you have two pairs or
more in the PAFOW."

"Your plan seems sound enough. I
will gather the heads of each growing
community. You can explain all of this to them
in the morning," Diplomat Mastinar (Mast)
replied.

"Then we will meet with them in the
morning. Thank you," I added with a bow.
We looked at Captain Elatron (Tron). He

nodded for us to leave. Captain Elatron (Tron) stayed and talked with Diplomat Mastinar (Mast).

Chapter Seven
Rescuing Ezethron (Zeth)

Elazephron (Laz) was busy making some of the parts he needed for his new engine design. Epsilon (Lonnie) was resting but not quite the way he wanted. Captain Elatron (Tron) had given him what we all called busy work to keep him out of trouble. So with some free time on our hands, Ezethron (Zeth) and I went to the Creation Domes. We decided to take a vacation of sorts to learn first-hand about the next planet we were to go to. We found that the information this planet had was the same as ours but we could see, hear and feel the information in the Creation Domes.

"Now, I think this is the best way to learn about anything," I said looking at Ezethron (Zeth).

"I agree. This would be a nice idea for our planet. I wonder if we could take the plans for one of these back with us when we go home?" came his reply.

"Wha! For what time period did you set the Domes' compulink?" I asked.

"I didn't really notice, but I have our wrist-compulinks," he said. "What was that?"

"It looks like you set it for prehistoric times," I commented. "I think you had better get us out of here or at least just set it so we are observers and not interacting," I suggested. But as life would have it, Ezethron (Zeth) was picked up and carried away by a very large bird before he could make the changes. As he was being carried away he threw one of the wrist-compulinks to me. I managed to find it in the middle of a large fern. I found out that wrist-compulinks wouldn't work unless we were both within a certain distance of each other and the same information needs to be entered on both for them to work. So I had my work cut out for me. Ezethron (Zeth) was lucky, it wasn't a meat-eating fowl that carried him off. I remember reading about the one that had flown away with him and it was a collector of things that were shiny, sort of like a packrat with wings. What a dilemma! I couldn't leave the program to go after the equipment I needed, like rope, lights, a knife and a weapon. And I couldn't create the things I needed because we were separated. If I tried to find the main compulink-panels, things could change in the program. Then I wouldn't know which way to hunt for Ezethron (Zeth) or what other beast might take him. So it looked like I was going to get a chance to put into practice everything I had ever learned about survival. Boy, what a challenge! After looking around and surveying my surroundings, I started out after Ezethron (Zeth).

"I hope for your sake you noticed which way you were being carried," I muttered to myself.

I had to remember to be very quiet because there were other beasts in this place that would love to have me for dinner and not as a guest. I moved very slowly through ferns and vines that were taller and bigger around than me. I was keeping a look out for other beasts, which I just had a feeling were very close. I made it a habit to look down before taking a step. Just in front of me, leaned up against a small tree, was a sharp shell about the size of my hand span. After I picked it up, I could see that someone had sharpened it. My first thoughts were that there must have been other humanoid life here during this time period.

I kept making my way through the thick undergrowth. The shell I had found was making travel much easier. After about what seemed like 10 milons (miles), I found a vine small enough in diameter and strong enough that I could use it as a rope. The vine was only about 15 lifnas (feet) long, but my thought was that by the time I needed it, I would find another piece and tie them together to make it longer.

I traveled for about another two decons (hours) before stopping for a rest. I sat down in some deep undergrowth so I wouldn't be spotted and eaten by some wild beast. While I sat there sucking on a piece of hardened juice that I always carried in my pockets. Hearing a yell, I pulled down a few leaves very quietly so I could hear better and figure out from which direction it was coming. It was Ezethron (Zeth)'s voice and he was just a short distance ahead and above me.

Getting up I quickened my pace as quietly as I could. After a few steps I heard the snap of branches behind me. I turned quickly to find this very curious looking humanoid standing in the middle of the path behind me. He was dressed in animal skins. He had dark matted hair, a short sparse beard, large black eyes, lightly tanned skin and was shorter than me (about four and one half lifnas (feet). I stood very still and just watched as he moved closer. He wasn't threatening but he was very curious. He reached out his small hand and touched the sleeve of the jumper I was wearing. Then he mumbled or hummed something and touched my hair. His words, or sounds for things, were almost like short two-note songs. Then my mind raced back to The People of Singing Words. I remembered a form of his language from what Grams taught me long ago, so I decided to try a few words. When I sang the word for "friend" and tried to relate my name his eyes lit up and a small smile came over his face.

He motioned to himself with the excitement of a small child with a new toy and sang, "Yahsang (Sang)" I took that to be his name. Then he motioned for me to follow him. So I followed. Just a short distance later I found myself in the middle of his tribal camp. In a matter of a few keptrons (minutes) I was surrounded by more of these short people. I studied the language for a few microns (seconds) using my side translator then decided to try and tell them what had happened to Ezethron (Zeth). I must have gotten the point across because they nodded at me, left for a few keptrons (minutes) and came back with everything we needed to climb to where the bird lived.

When we left their camp, one of the stronger looking men had taken a long rope and shell that had been polished to a high shine. He stood in the middle of a clearing and bounced the light rays off the shell. It wasn't long before the large bird came and flew off with him, too.

I just stood there following the bird with my eyes and though it must have been Ezethron (Zeth)'s metallic shirt that caught the bird's eye. Then one of the men tapped me on the shoulder. I looked back over my shoulder at him. The rest of the hunting party motioned for me to follow them, so I did.

It wasn't long before we were at the bottom of a high plateau. When we looked up to the top we could see a large nest with a long vine rope hanging from it. One of the men in the hunting party was very good at climbing, so up he went with even more vine rope over his shoulders. He had a strange way of holding himself in place on the cliff wall when he needed both hands free. He had a set of large bird claws attached to a woven vine rope, which he placed in a slit in the cliff face, and the other end he tied around himself. While he hung from the side of the cliff he tied the vine rope he had brought up with him to the vine rope that was hanging over from the nest. After he had finished tying the vines together he gave them a yank, to let those in the nest know that they had a way down.

Meanwhile, one of the hunters had set out a few more of the shiny shells hoping to lure the big bird out of the nest, so Ezethron (Zeth) and the other hunter could climb over the edge to come down, they made sure to leave the shell and Ezethron (Zeth)'s shirt in the nest so that the bird wouldn't miss them. Before long they were both on the ground with the rest of us.

I introduced Ezethron (Zeth) to the rest of the tribe and we said our good-byes and left the Creation Dome after saving the program.

Once outside, I scolded Ezethron (Zeth), "Don't you ever set the compulink to just go anywhere in any time period!"

"Oh relax, will you? We got out of it okay, didn't we?" Ezethron (Zeth) said with a smile and almost a chuckle. "I made sure there weren't any dangerous beasts in the program before I started it."

"Yeah, well, you're mean, really mean sometimes. I was really worried about you. You're just a real monkey bag full of tricks," I said as I relaxed. It was hard to stay angry with Ezethron (Zeth).

Looking at my timelink, I took a deep breath "We had better get back to the lab so we can get set up for in the morning's experiment and the people we have to teach."

"Yes, I guess you're right," Ezethron (Zeth) agreed, still laughing. "You mean I really had you going? You really thought there were dangerous beasts in that program?"

"Yes, I did," I said, still acting angry with him.

"I wouldn't ever purposely put either of us in danger. You know that don't you?" Ezethron (Zeth) asked, looking at me seriously.

"I do now. But you are such a tease that sometimes I'm not sure if you think things out completely," I said with a big grin.

By the time we got everything set up for the next sestrons (days) experiment it was time to go to the next meal. Then there would be just enough time to relax before going to sleep.

Chapter Eight
Crash Landing Sadness

The next morning found us feeling great after a good night's sound sleep. We met with the heads of each growing area and explained how the two parts of the experiment would work.

The next three sestrons (days) were spent helping them set up the equipment. We stayed on the planet for a few more pestrons (weeks) so we could monitor the experiments and make sure that everyone knew what they were doing.

Elazephron (Laz) finished the engine modifications he had been working on.

"Hi, Elazephron (Laz), explain to me how this new engine of yours is supposed to help us?" I asked as I came on board our craft and entered the engine room.

"Do you want the short version or the long one?" he asked with a big grin.

"Spare me the lecture and just give me the short version," I said with a chuckle.

"Okay. Well, to make it short, this new design will help us move into the time dimension for our travel time. In other words, it won't take us as long to get where we are going. Okay? Short enough?" Elazephron (Laz) said with a big grin.

"Yeah, really good, you know you're getting better at giving short versions," I said laughing as I turned and walked out of the room.

Within the next few pestrons (weeks) we were all back on board our ship and on the way to our next mission, Planet 3/2SS (Earth as it is known to its inhabitants).

I was busy helping Ezethron (Zeth) sort the data we had just gathered, when our ship suddenly shook. I got up from my work and went to the doors that shut us off from the bridge. When I opened the doors my ears were bombarded by a wave of confusion. Through all the noise of the compulink's information coming in, I could hear Engineer

Elazephron (Laz) reporting, "Minor damage to our forward sensors, Sir!"

"How bad?" asked Captain Elatron (Tron).

"Won't know for a few more microns (seconds), Sir!" Elazephron (Laz) reported.

"How are the visuals, Epsilon (Lonnie)?" Captain Elatron (Tron) shouted over the compulink noise as he turned around in his chair.

"Readable, Sir, just minor damage," Epsilon (Lonnie) reported.

Just then Ezethron (Zeth) walked up behind me and leaned through door to the bridge. "Any injuries?" he asked, loudly.

"Everyone is okay here Ezethron (Zeth)," I said.

"Good! Good!" And with that, Ezethron (Zeth) went back into his test papers. (Ezethron (Zeth) was always running tests on the DNA of plants and small animals he would gather.)

A few keptrons (minutes) later everything settled down and seemed to be running smoothly.

"Captain Elatron (Tron), what caused the problems?" I asked as I stepped outside the lab doors.

"We ran into some sort of debris that didn't show on our sensors," said Captain Elatron (Tron) looking at Epsilon (Lonnie).

I went back to my duties in the lab. A few microns (seconds) later as we entered the atmosphere of Earth, I was urged by inner feelings to strap myself into my console chair. I didn't know at this time why I got that feeling, but I knew better than to go against it. I gave the compulink the command to open the door to the bridge and as I stood there and looking through the data I had collected, this feeling of urgency swept over me again.

"Captain Elatron (Tron). Please have everyone strap in!" I relayed my feelings. Before the captain could answer, a cloud of confusion once again swept over the ship.

"Captain," shouted Epsilon (Lonnie), "visuals are gone!"

"Completely?" I heard the Captain ask.

"We are flying blind except for our sensors!" Epsilon (Lonnie)'s shouted over the noise.

"No! The sensors are all off-line, too!" screamed Elazephron (Laz) in the confusion. "Our engines just went off-line, too, Captain! We are flying like a rock through this planet's atmosphere!"

At that, the Captain shouted, "Strap in! We're going down!"

Everyone scrambled for their chairs, but didn't get to them in time because we were now hitting things and being tossed about in the ship. I figured it was trees by the sound of it. Then everything went black and silent.

When I regained consciousness, I could hear the faint hum of the emergency lights and life support systems. I heard scrambling from some of the cages in Ezethron (Zeth)'s lab. I checked myself for injuries. I seemed to be okay outside of bruises from the straps. I unbuckled my safety harness and managed to get my footing. I went to check the Captain, then to Epsilon (Lonnie). They were both dead. Then

I heard a grunting noise coming from what seemed to be under one of the center consoles. It was there on the floor, that I found Elazephron (Laz) pinned between a console and the captain's chair.

"How badly are you hurt?" I asked.

"I'm not sure at this point. Help me get this console off of me so I'm free; then I can tell more," Elazephron (Laz) replied. As we started to move the console, "Stop!" he cried out. "I'm feeling a stabbing sensation in my chest."

"Oh, this thing is heavier than I thought. Wait a keptron (minute). Let me get something to pry it off of you," I said as I frantically looked around for something to use.

"Oh! Uh, sharp chest pains." he groaned. AH! UH!" Then he was silent.

"I found something to use," I announced. Then I noticed that his eyes were closed. I sat down beside him for a short while and cried. I guess I didn't really know until that micron (second) how much I really had loved him. As I stroked his brow, I found myself talking to him. "Please, Elazephron

(Laz), don't leave me now; not this way, I love you. You can't leave, please, Please don't leave me!" As I cried, half-pleading and half-praying, a tear had dropped onto his face.

"I love you, too, and I'll always be with you. Our love is joined," he said as he opened his eyes and looked at me one last time. With his hand he gently touched my cheek and then he closed his eyes and died, his hand dropping to his chest.

I thought my heart was breaking into pieces. I felt lost, trapped, fearful, angry, and a deep sense of loss all at the same time. I felt so confused and lonely. Then from a small opening in the lab door I heard a faint moaning. The door was jammed. I picked up the piece of metal I was going to free Elazephron (Laz) with and pried the door open enough to get through it.

One of the lab tables had fallen on Ezethron (Zeth).

He motioned to me with his free hand. "Lift the table off," his words were, hard to make out.

It took a while, but the table finally went upright.

"Eze, can you hear me?" I asked.

"Yes," he replied in a low weak voice.

"Where are you hurt?" I asked.

"All over; mostly inside I think. It hurts really bad to move. I must be bleeding inside. I'm really thirsty. Get that meter with the wand over there and run it over me and show me the readout," he said in a low forced voice while trying to point.

As I passed the meter over his broken body, I could feel the pain in his spirit and it was becoming seeable in his face.

"Okay. What does it say?" I asked showing him the readout. It seemed like decons (hours) before he answered.

"Worse than I thought, I may have about two decons (hours) at most. I have major internal injuries and massive bleeding." And then he lost consciousness. I stayed with him, but he never came to again. He died just a little while after he passed out.

It took me some time to get my head straight and my emotions under control. After all, I had just lost all of my teammates, my love, my best friend and my only way of getting back home--all at the same time.

I turned on the interstellar homing signal. Then I gathered up what supplies I could find, zipped up my jacket and pried open the outer door of the ship. Our people had visited this planet before so I knew the air was good and there was plenty of water and food. "Wow! What a landing," I thought to myself aloud. The ship was lodged in the side of a mountain some 20 lifnas (feet) above a ledge. "Well, the only way out is down." So after lowering all of the supplies I would need, I climbed down the tether lines.

When on the ground, I took mental note of everything I had gathered. I had warm clothing, a shelter, medical supplies, food supplements, a few personal belongings, my side translator and my Crystal Array Kayits. I knew the inhabitants of this planet were humanoid like me, except that my people refused to kill except in extreme cases of emergency.

I was in luck. There was a good place near where I climbed down from the ship to set up camp. I had just put the last piece of equipment into place when I heard a rustling in the bushes nearby. I knew I was being watched from the beginning, but there wasn't any sound until now. I had a chance to study the plants in the area and from what I learned back at the academy, I knew I was on the mid-eastern coast of the northern section of the second largest land mass or somewhere close, because I had found May Apples. Unless things had changed a lot, the people in this area were of a light brown skin and very curious and friendly. I got out the windpipe Grams had given me and started playing the songs she had taught. Flute music had always seemed to bring them out of the bushes according to Grams.

Chapter Nine
Myawop - Indians?

Four young braves approached me cautiously but curious. With the help of my side translator and after talking to them for a while, their language started to sound familiar. I learned that one was called Tall Grass, another was Running Elk, Strong Bow was the chief's son and Bent Twig was the medicine man's son. Tall Grass was the tallest of the braves at a little over six lifnas (feet) and Bent Twig was the smallest and shortest at around five and one-half lifnas (feet).

It seemed that they had seen the "star" fall from the heavens and came to see what God had given them. I was finding it a great relief that my people had interfaced with these people before, and that I had a chance to study the language before I left on this trip. They wanted me to come back to their camp with them. I explained to them I needed to bury my dead friends and they agreed to help me. But it was getting late, and night would soon be upon us, so we would wait until morning to bury them.

We built a campfire and laid down. I tried to sleep, but I found myself looking up at the stars and wishing I could get a message back to my home planet. Then the thought hit me; there just might be a chance that a passing visitor may hear the interstellar homing signal from our ship and report it to the United Planets Alliance. I breathed a sigh of relief and fell into a deep sleep and dreamt of some of the good times I'd had with my friends when we were younger.

I was awakened by Tall Grass at dawn's first light. "Your friends must travel while it is light to find their way back to the place of their grandfathers," he said softly. So with his help and the help of the others, we set up pulleys to get the other crew members out of the ship. They were buried as

I requested after I explained our burial customs.

After my team members were buried, the braves helped me carry all of the things I was taking back to their camp. Strong Bow went on ahead of us and let his people know what they had found, and to tell them about me.

As we neared their camp, some of the people came out to greet us. I was accepted like an old friend. They carried some of my things for me and by the time I got to the center of their camp I wasn't carrying anything.

"Ah, White Dove," came a greeting from somewhere. I looked around to see who was speaking. Then after studying the crowd, I learned that it was me who was being called White Dove. I wondered why the name "White Dove," then I looked at myself a little closer and realized I was wearing a white metallic jump suit. My guess was the name came from what I was wearing and how I arrived here. (Most of these people were named after something they did or saw at the time of one's birth.)

As I came closer to the Chief's tent, I knew that this greeting had come from him.

"This is Running Bear, our chief and my father," Strong Bow said.

Chief Running Bear was a tall, strong looking man with well-groomed buckskin clothing, long black hair and almost black eyes. He looked to be in his early forties. I knew by now after talking to the young braves and hearing the rest of the tribe talk, that these were The People of The Wind, I felt lucky. This was one of the languages that Grams had taught me.

I looked at Chief Running Bear and nodded my head. "I come in peace." I told him holding out both of my hands with my palms up.

Taking me by the hand gently, Chief Running Bear said, "I will take you to Two Wolves and Healing Water, you will be in their care." And we walked farther into the camp.

"Two Wolves! Come out and meet White Dove," Chief Running Bear called out.

Two Wolves opened his tent door and stuck out his head first to see who called for him. Then in a flash he was standing in front of me, looking me over, up and down. Then his wife, Healing Waters, set me at ease. Two Wolves was a stern looking man at first glance; strong and rugged looking. He was about the same height as the chief, but he wore his hair with two small braids, one over each ear decorated with stone beads and feathers, the rest of his hair was sprawled out over his broad shoulders. His wife, Healing Waters, on the other hand, was about my height and a little heavy. She wore two braids like her husband, but her long black braids were farther back almost in back of her ears and the rest of her hair was tied back with a strip of deer hide. When Two Wolves and Healing Waters looked at me, it felt like they were looking at my soul.

"White Dove will be staying with you. Make her welcome," Running Bear said. Then he turned and left me standing at their tent door with everything I had brought with me.

"Come put your things over here," Healing Waters said softly while looking curiously at me then she continued. "You came from the skies? Have you a message from the Great Creator?"

"No, I'm not a messenger. I'm just a visitor. I'm here to learn your ways and to report to my people on how you are doing," I answered the best I could.

"You may sleep here tonight," she said pointing to a corner of their tent. "Tomorrow we will help make you a better place." I was nearly of marrying age by their laws and since I wasn't one of their children, I would be adopted into Two Wolves household till I married.

I helped Healing Waters gather firewood, start a campfire and cook dinner that night. I had studied some of their customs before coming to Earth. And I knew that taking care of everything in camp dealing with the good of the people was the women's job. If a job was too hard for one woman to take care of then all of the women in the camp worked on it as a team. I felt that I was no different now, that I was going to be part of the tribe. For right now they were my people.

Two Wolves, Bent Twig, Healing Waters and I sat around the campfire after the meal and the chores were done that evening. It was then that I had a chance to show them some of the things I had brought with me.

The next morning when I awoke, Healing Waters and Two Wolves were just coming back from a meeting with Running Bear. It seems that they had all gotten together and decided I was to become Two Wolves' and Healing Waters' daughter. Bent Twig was standing there looking at me with a big smile on his face.

"I will have a sister," he said while nodding his head. "You already have the name of White Dove and now you will have a family here," he added pointing to the ground.

After a whirlwind of events and ceremonies, I was now the daughter of Two Wolves and Healing Waters and the sister of Bent Twig.

I learned quickly which combinations of herbs were needed for the different illnesses that my Earth family was most likely to suffer. There were times when I was sent looking for herbs and Bent Twig came along to hunt, so he said. But most of the time, if there was water nearby I would find him looking into it and sestron (day) dreaming. I always kept that as a secret because he wasn't in the best of health. I was glad to have him come with me. This way I knew he was safe.

His body was bent from a childhood injury and his lungs were weak, and we had become very close as time went by.

Almost a secto (year) had passed since I had crashed on Earth.

I always had my Crystal Array Kayits (CAK) with me and Bent Twig knew it. He was becoming known as a good hunter. He would spot a rabbit, I would stun it with my CAK and while it was out, he would kill it and we would take it home. This had gone on for a few mistrons (months). Then, one sestron (day) while we were out gathering May Apples and berries, Bent Twig found some bees. He went over to gather the honey, but didn't notice the black bear who had also wanted the honey. All of a sudden he was being attacked.

While he was screaming and the scuffle was going on, it was hard to hit just the bear with my CAK. Finally, out of desperation, I set the gun on heavy stun and fired at the bear hoping I would miss Bent Twig. The bear went down on top of Bent Twig. After some hard pulling and pushing I managed to move the bear off of Bent Twig. He was near death. The bear had caused some major injuries. His stomach had been ripped open and he was rapidly losing blood. I held him in my arms and talked quietly to him.

"I'm going to go see Grandfather Owl soon. Promise me that you will look after Mom and Dad," he implored softly.

"Yes, I will take care of them the best I can," I promised with tears in my eyes.

Just then the bear started to gain consciousness so I shot him again, this time with my CAK set on kill.

"You will be known as a great hunter little brother. I will see to that." I looked down at him and with a small smile he died.

I laid him down and went to work on the bear. I had to make it look like my brother had won even though he had died in the process. I was determined his death wasn't going to be in vain.

I made a travois and managed to drag both the bear and my little brother back to camp.

When I got to the edge of camp, Healing Waters saw me coming and knew that something was wrong when she didn't see her son.

She ran towards me, more of the women joined her. She looked at me. I looked at her, then over my shoulder to the travois.

At that point she started to wail as was their tradition. All the other women joined her. I was given help dragging Bent Twig and the bear the rest of the way into camp. After Healing Waters settled down and things were calmer, I related to her and the rest of the tribe the story of a great fight, and how Bent Twig was a great hunter and warrior for courageously killing the bear. I told of the possibilities of it coming into camp and causing trouble if it wasn't for Bent Twig's heroic victory over the bear.

Bent Twig was given a great hunter's funeral ceremony. And that made me happy.

Chapter Ten
Waiting

Sectos (years) had passed since the crash, and I still found myself looking at the stars every night; looking, waiting and wondering if my interstellar homing signal would ever be heard. I would go back to my ship every once in a while to check on things and to make sure that the note I left for the search team was still in place.

I remember sitting by the camp fire one evening during one of the many celebrations we had, just looking up at the skies when..... "I'm not really sure, but I think I just saw a ship coming into the atmosphere. Oh, God, I hope it's a ship, I would really love to hear from my birth home again." I thought.

Standing up to get a better look, Strong Bow spotted me looking into the skies, and moved closer to me.

"What do you see?" he asked me in a low voice so as not to alert the others.

I looked back at him, "I think maybe my people have found me."

"Does that mean you will be going back to your home?" he asked with disappointment in his voice.

"Yes," I said looking into his eyes.

When he reached over and gathered my hands into his and looking into my eyes. He said "I was going to ask you to be my wife later this evening. I have already asked Two Wolves and Healing Waters and they have given me their permission."

Now at this point I felt really torn. I loved being with Strong Bow and becoming his wife sounded really good to me. But at the same time I wanted to go home if I had a chance. "I would love to be your wife, but I want to go home to be with my people, too. Can you understand this?" I asked, hoping for a yes answer.

"Yes, I understand how you feel, but we don't know if those are your home world people," he offered. "Please. Let's go and give the good news to our parents now."

"Well, okay," I said sort of hesitant, not knowing if that was a ship that had come in or not. I realized that I had to live as my real Dad had taught me, "Prepare for life like you are going to live for thousands of sectos (years) and live life as if you are going to die in keptrons (minutes)".

So off we went to tell our families the good news.

The next morning everyone woke up early. We had a lot of preparation to do before the joining. By late afternoon I was free to do what I wanted. So I headed back to my ship. I had to know, if what I had seen the night before was really a rescue party looking for me. I went to the crash site and saw that someone had landed. But I didn't recognize the ship design.

Hiding patiently in the bushes I waited to see who these people were. After what seemed to be a long time, I spotted a humanoid coming up from the creek bed. He was strange looking to me, but of course I didn't know all the races in the United Planets Alliance.

Then I saw another humanoid coming from the other direction. When they spoke to each other I was able to make out about every third word or so. Maybe they were looking for me. Maybe they had heard my signal.

I came out of the bushes and greeted them. I told them my story and found out that they couldn't take me back with them. They just wanted to make sure I was still alive before they sent for a rescue party.

They told me they had one of the older ships and it would take a while for them to get close enough to my solar system to send a message.

"How long do you think that will take you?" I asked.

They looked at each other, then answered, "It will take about seven mistrons (months) to get close enough to your solar system to send a message, once we finish our mission. And we can't tell you how long it will be before your people send out a ship for you."

"Well, just give the message to them that I am alive, I love them, and that I want to come home. I will be waiting for them, okay?"

"Okay. We will give them your message as soon as we can. Bye," they said as they climbed back aboard their ship and prepared to take off.

I waved and left. On my way back to camp I met Strong Bow headed toward my ship. He had been looking for me. "I thought you decided to go with your friends, but I am glad you are still here," he said while giving me a hug.

"No, I mean, yes. But they didn't have room for us on their ship. So, all I did was to talk to them and explain what had happened so far," I said smiling at him. "They will send a message to my people, so they can come for us," I continued.

He wrapped his arm around me and we went back to camp.

Thirteen mistrons (months) after
Strong Bow and I were married, we had a
son. We gave him the name Elmosa (Mosa),
which would have been my name for him on
my home planet and his tribal name of
Singing Wolf.

Our son was a little over two sectos
(years) old when I saw another ship come
into the atmosphere one evening. I told
Strong Bow about the ship that night.

The next morning we got up, gathered
our son and went back to my ship. As we
approached the old crash site, I could see
that the people were from my home planet. I
thought I recognized one of them, but it
couldn't be who I thought it was. I mean,
Master Enahsto (Master E) was well up in
sectos (years) before I had left on the
mission. As I got closer, I called out, "Master
Enahsto (Master E), is that you?" The person
turned around to face me.

"No, I am Master Enahsto (Master E)'s
sintho. He could not make the trip himself
because of his age, so he sent me instead. He
said to tell you, he thought you would like to
see a familiar face in the landing party, so

here I am," the sintho said. "I am known as Enah 2 (E2). I am the Captain of this mission."

Then one of the other crewmembers came over to talk to me. He was a little strange looking: he was very well built, standing a little over six lifnas (feet) tall with a slight blue tint to his skin. He was wearing a United Planets Alliance uniform, but he must be from another planet in the U. P.A. His pointed ears looked odd as they extended above his black thickly frizzed hair. Standing there smiling, with his large dark eyes seeming to sparkle.

"Hi! I am called Meninso. There have been many changes in the Alliance since you have been gone. Now our search and rescue groups are of mixed races from various planets. We all live as exchange trainees on other planets. This way we learn of other cultures first hand. Good idea, yes?" he asked with a big smile. Then he caught sight of Elmosa (Mosa) peeking around my shoulder from his father's arms.

"Oh, a small person, hello!" he said as he reached out to take Elmosa (Mosa)'s hand very gently.

Elmosa (Mosa) looked up at Meninso and laughed. Then Elmosa (Mosa) did the unexpected. He reached out for Meninso. Meninso took Elmosa (Mosa) from his father's arms as I nodded my okay. Meninso then carried Elmosa (Mosa) up the landing ramp while pointing at the bright colors.

"We are going to be good friends, really good friends," he said as he bounced Elmosa (Mosa) in his arms and they both laughed.

Strong Bow and I followed them into the ship and looked to see how much space it had. I wanted to see if there was enough room to take home some gifts.

Enah 2 (E2) seemed to know what I was thinking. "Yes, there is room for presents and keepsakes. But you had better hurry. We want to catch the right orbital opening. We have three decons (hours) and forty-three keptrons (minutes) before we must take off," he said as he gently pushed us towards the door. I turned and looked at

Strong Bow. He was in a state of wonder, eyes opened wide and mouth slightly agape.

As we stepped out onto the ramp of the ship I saw most of the tribe coming up the path. It became clear that Strong Bow had told his parents about the ship and us leaving. Many of them were carrying our belongings and gifts. The ones who were bringing things, stepped forward and put them on the ramp in front of us. So we stood at the base of the ship and said our good-byes for now. Strong Bow tried telling the tribe about the many different peoples our Creator had created. I motioned for Meninso and Enah 2 (E2) to come out. Everyone looked up, gasped and backed away a step or two, then noticed Elmosa (Mosa) in Meninso's arms and breathed easier.

Running Bear stepped forward with a big smile and held out his hands to Meninso and Enah 2 (E2). "Now we have many kinds of friends," Everyone laughed and nodded.

Chapter Eleven
People from U.P.A.

Meninso put Elmosa (Mosa) down and started helping Enah 2 (E2) and I carry the bundles into the ship. Strong Bow went and talked to his parents and said his good-byes to his grandparents. Two Wolves and Healing Waters asked if they could see the inside of the ship. Enah 2 (E2) gave his okay and I brought them in while Meninso entertained Elmosa (Mosa).

Two Wolves first stood at the door, wide eyed in astonishment.

"This is all most amazing," spoke up Healing Waters.

"Come. Let me show you where we will sleep on the way to my other home," I said taking them both by the hand.

"Ah, so soft," Healing Waters said as she pressed on the bed, "and such wonderful colors like a rainbow and many flowers all together."

"This is all good medicine," piped up Two Wolves once he found his voice. It wasn't often he was without words.

"Oh yes, there is an area that I want to show you both," I said, thinking of the medical area. On the way we had to pass through the bridge. "This is where we drive the ship. See? We are able to see outside even without openings in the walls." I said pointing at the view screen.

"Yes," Two Wolves said, as he went up to touch the picture of what he thought was outside. When he reached out to touch what he thought was the tribe standing outside, his hand went through the holographic field and the image scattered for a micron (second), then it resumed its pattern.

Being fascinated with the screen, he hadn't noticed that someone was sitting at the console in the large full body chair next to where he was standing.

"Ahh!" Two Wolves gasped and jumped back as the chair turned showing the third crewmember of the rescue party.

"Oh, I am Paleeto (Pal). I am from Tanose in the sixth solar system from Elaytay (Tay)'s home planet. I am the navigator for this trip," Paleeto (Pal) explained, trying to put Two Wolves and Strong Bow at ease.

Standing up so we could see him better, he bowed. Paleeto (Pal) was only five lifnas (feet) tall, had light creamy skin, larger than average head, longer than average fingers and large almond-shaped black eyes. We learned that Paleeto (Pal) and his people are usually of very few spoken words.

"That was very good, Paleeto (Pal). When you introduced yourself, you spoke in Strong Bow's language. Where did you learn their language?" I asked. Noticing he didn't have a translator on him.

"I learn languages very fast because I pick them up from others' thoughts," explained Paleeto (Pal). "I said this right?" he questioned, raising one eyebrow.

"Yes, that was said right," I answered with a smile.

Paleeto (Pal) looked at me and smiled slightly. I turned to Two Wolves and Healing Waters and explained to them that there are others from far away planets who talk with thoughts and use very little or no spoken words or sounds. Two Wolves nodded that he understand and Healing Waters just smiled and looked at Paleeto (Pal). Paleeto (Pal) let out a small giggle as he and Healing Waters communicated telepathically. "I am pleased. This is great. Not only did our people meet each other, but now there is complete communication," I observed. And with that, Healing Waters and Paleeto (Pal) both nodded and smiled.

"Your knowledge is great, and I am glad that I had this chance to learn from you," Healing Waters said and smiled at Paleeto (Pal).

As we turned around, I pointed out the medical bay and lab. "This is where we help the ones who get sick or hurt," I said.

Enah 2 (E2) came back into the ship with Elmosa (Mosa).

We all looked at Enah 2 (E2), "Elmosa (Mosa) has been showing me some of the fowl in the area, but it is now time for our departure, so all that are to stay on this planet must leave the ship," he announced.

"Okay," I acknowledged with a nod. Then I turned back to Two Wolves and Healing Waters. "We will come back and bring you some of our medical plants. We will try to return by the 10th deer hunt." I put my hand out and pointed towards the door. I walked with them to the ramp.

When we all got to the bottom of the ramps, everyone stood silent for a few microns (seconds). "This is only a "see you later". I don't like good-byes; they seem so final," I reached out and hugged them both.

"Till next we meet again," said Two Wolves.

"Yes, and our love goes with you," added Healing Waters.

And with that we both followed Enah 2 (E2) up the ramp to the ship door. At the top we all waved.

After the door closed and we all strapped in. Everyone outside the ship stepped back about 20 paces, to clear the ignition area, as instructed by Chief Running Bear. We could see all of them on the view screen as we lifted off.

Tears of happiness and sadness accumulated in my eyes and as one rolled down my cheek, Strong Bow reached out and softly swept it from my face.

"What's the matter? Are you sick or in pain?" he asked in concern.

"No, I'm feeling mixed emotions. Part of me is happy to be going back to be with my birth family and at the same time part of me is sad to be leaving my Earth family," I replied.

"Oh! I understand, yes," Strong Bow said in a relaxed, but thoughtful tone.

Getting farther out into space, I got a chance to settle back for the journey to my birth home. Strong Bow and I could hear Elmosa (Mosa) giggling from another part of the ship.

Meninso had completed his duties for the time being and was keeping Elmosa (Mosa) entertained. I got up and walked over to where they were.

I could see that Meninso had the holographic theater on, and that was what Elmosa (Mosa) was laughing at. He was watching a holographic movie of the animals of other planets. The holographic movies always seemed so real to me. They came complete with sights, sounds, and smells and were fed to the brain through the helmet-type headgear. The head gear was run by a compulink which arranged the out-put signals to the proper sites of the brain according to the user's race, and age so it could best translate the signals.

"Have you seen this movie?" Meninso inquired.

As I looked at the movie, I answered, "No. Where are these animals found?"

Meninso loved to study animals and plants so he was full of answers for me. "We now have all these animals on your home planet," he added.

"Oh?" I questioned.

"Yes! After your scout ship left and the okay was given to collect DNA samples for cloning, we had other ships bring back DNA samples and the less threatening species were cloned with great success. Some of them turned out to be very smart when put in the right environment," he added.

"I can hardly wait to see them," I said excitedly.

"You do understand that some of these are still in holding centers being studied?" he asked as he looked over at me.

I nodded, as I watched Elmosa (Mosa)'s actions towards what he was seeing. Elmosa (Mosa) gazed at the holographic screen as if he was in a trance. I reached over and touched his shoulder, "Look, Mama! Look! See? "Elmosa (Mosa) said clapping his small hands and looking up at me. Then a sound and smell caught his attention again, "Pretty!" He giggled out loud as he wiggled in his chair.

"Yes, they are nice. When we get to our new home, maybe we can go see some of these for real. Okay?" I announced.

"Yes, yes, yes," Elmosa (Mosa) said loudly while clapping his hands.

By that time, Strong Bow had joined us to see what all the commotion was about. So I explained what was happening and he smiled and went back to where he was sitting.

We were traveling through the stars at that point.

Meninso continued to entertain Elmosa (Mosa), so I went back to sit down beside Strong Bow.

Enah 2 (E2) was explaining the different heavenly formations we could see at that time.

Strong Bow looked up at me as I sat down and strapped in. "I didn't know that the skies had so many names. Where is the sun? Why is it so dark outside? Is it night-time?" he asked as his questions seemed to bubble out like a spring.

"Whoa, slow down. Don't try to learn everything in such a short time. There is plenty of time to learn all of this," I explained with a smile. "Now one question at a time, okay?" I added.

"Okay, so why is it so dark out here?" he asked as his gaze returned to the view screen.

"Well, to put it in terms that I think you will understand easier, do you remember how we used to have more than one campfire in our camp?" I asked waiting for some kind of acknowledgment.

"Yes, so?" Strong Bow finally said with a nod.

"Well, do you remember how dark it was between campfires?" I prodded farther.

He nodded again, "So?"

"Okay, well try to imagine in your mind that the suns are the different campfires. Right now we are between suns, so it's dark outside just like it is between campfires," I said, hoping he understood.

"Oh!" he said.

"Do you understand what I just explained?" I asked.

"Well, sort of, but, I don't see any other sun. Where are they?" Strong Bow questioned.

Enah 2 (E2) piped in, "At the point we are in space, excuse me what you call the sky of heavens, all of the suns look just like stars. Actually, stars and suns are the same thing for the most part."

"Oh! So the stars we were looking at on Earth are called suns, but far away," Strong Bow said, seeming to understand.

"Yes! Yes! Now you have it," I said excitedly.

"But some change sizes and some don't. Why?" Strong Bow asked anxiously.

"Well, that may be a little harder to explain, but I will try," I said while searching for an explanation that would be easy to understand.

"Okay. You know when you put wood into a fire and the sap sometimes causes a bigger flame at times than it does at other times?" I asked.

"Yes, so," came Strong Bows reply.

"Well a star is on fire and gets that kind of energy bursts just like campfires. That is why suns and campfires seem to change size and shape," I explained. "Some suns are very old and their fire begins to cool, just like a campfire that is left to die out. As a sun cools, there are no more burst of energy to make it change size or shape."

"Okay, but why is it that some of these don't change size?" he asked.

"Well, these are planets and are not on fire like the stars. They just bounce off the light from the sun they are near, like the sunlight bouncing off the water of a quiet lake" I continued.

"Well, why are some stars, suns?" he asked unexpectedly.

"Think of the large campfire in the middle of our camp with the members of our tribe dancing around it, and that star in the middle of the planets is like the campfire with the dancers. That star is called a sun because it has planets going around it," I tried to explain.

"Okay," came the response from Strong Bow then he went back to watching the view screen.

Chapter Twelve
Near Miss

Soon it came time to eat and I knew that this should prove to be an experience not soon forgotten.

"Strong Bow," Enah 2 (E2) said addressing him, holding out a small tray of different shaped containers. Strong Bow looked up at Enah 2 (E2) and took the tray then looked at me.

"This is our meal," I explained to Strong Bow as Enah 2 (E2) handed me one too, "On a small ship like this one we have what is known as pressed foods because of the shortage of storage space. Don't worry, it tastes good and most of the time the texture is the same as the real thing. The fowl has the texture of real meat, not soft like cereal.

Look. On each container is the name of what it is, okay?" I explained.

"Ok, but I don't understand these markings yet so I will need help." Strong Bow's words brought back forgotten details. Of course he didn't know how to read. Nothing was ever written down in words on Earth, at least not by his people.

"Yes, of course, love. I'm sorry I had forgotten. I will be more than glad to read them to you, and later if you want I will show you even more about reading," I explained.

"What is reading? And why must I learn it?" asked Strong Bow.

"You will need to learn to read because I may want to tell you something when I'm not around. And in that case I will write some of these symbols on something and they will tell you where I am." I explained. "Like this," I said pointing to the tray of food. "These marking tell us that this is a fruit drink." I went on to explain what we were eating and drinking.

Time seemed to fly by. Strong Bow had learned to read quite a few words of my world before it was time to sleep.

Elmosa (Mosa) gave out early and fell asleep in the chair while he was watching the animals in the holographic theater. After putting Elmosa (Mosa) in his bunk, I walked to our quarters with Strong Bow. We both snuggled in and fell asleep almost immediately.

Our sleeping time went by rapidly and the next thing I remembered was Elmosa (Mosa) at the end of our bed tugging on the cover. Strong Bow sat up in bed, looked at Elmosa (Mosa) and put out his arms. Elmosa (Mosa) promptly took that as an invitation and crawled up in the middle of us giggling.

"So, what are you up to so early, my son?" Strong Bow asked as he played with Elmosa (Mosa).

Elmosa (Mosa) giggled even more and pointed to the other room.

"Okay, we will get up and you can show us what you want to do," Strong Bow responded as he got out of bed.

We both got dressed and went into the main part of the ship.

Elmosa (Mosa) went running to the other side of the ship, close to where he had been the sestron (day) before. He climbed into and sat down in this large chair and motioned for his father to come and join him. Strong Bow went over and sat down. Meninso came over and explained to Strong Bow how the console on the arm of the chair worked. Elmosa (Mosa) and he sat there for the biggest part of the sestron (day) watching the holographic movie explaining parts of the planet that they would be living on for the next 10 sectos (years).

Meanwhile, I had a chance to show Enah 2 (E2) the samples of DNA I had collected in the time that I was on Earth. "I got a few DNA samples of horses, rabbits, birds, opossum, different birds, fish and a few others including the squirrel. So, what do you think, Enah 2 (E2)?" I asked eagerly.

"I'm not sure. Let's run a few tests on the samples you have and we will know if they can be cloned. Did you get samples from a male and female of each specimen?" he asked.

"I tried but with some of the birds I couldn't tell what gender they were so I just collected what I could," I said with a smile.

"Yes, with some species it is hard to tell which is which. So we will work with what we have and hope for the best," Enah 2 (E2) replied.

We ran tests most of the sestron (day). The majority of the samples I had collected on Earth were good to use for cloning. Then we ran tests on the DNA Sample Containers we had gathered on the first planet we had visited before the crash. Some of them were okay but some were lost because the solar generated isolating chambers had been damaged in the crash.

I was relieved to know that all of the work that Ezethron (Zeth) and I had done wasn't lost. If I'd had my way at the time of Ezethron (Zeth)'s death I would have gathered a DNA sample of the crewmembers, but that was against the laws of the United Planets Alliance. And now, thinking back on that, it wouldn't have been right. It would have been torment for their families, not to mention myself. As it is we all have our memories of them and how they were.

As the sestrons (days), pestrons (weeks) and mistrons (months) passed, Strong Bow learned to read our written language, learned our customs and ways of life.

Elmosa (Mosa) began learning to read very well, but like most children, he liked pictures best. He learned the games and ways of children on my home planet. For being a little less than three secto (year) old he was very smart.

I was told that we now have a very well integrated planet. Our planet is now culturally well blended. Enah 2 (E2) made sure that I knew the ways of some of the new planets that had joined the Alliance during my absence. There was plenty we all had to learn before we got back to my home planet, so all three of us remained busy.

Then one morning, we were awakened from a sound sleep with the rushing sound of hurried computations.

"Captain, I'm picking up the indication of space debris," came Paleeto (Pal)'s thoughts as clear as if he had said them aloud in a quiet room.

Enah 2 (E2) answered aloud, "Paleeto (Pal), evasive maneuvers! Keep us clear of all of it, and slow to a quarter of our speed. I want more information on the debris."

"Yes, Sir!" came back Paleeto (Pal)'s response, aloud.

By that time I was sitting at one of the data centers. After Paleeto (Pal) and I ran the computations on the debris, we found it had been a ship, but it had no known markings. "With the data we have, the debris is of a ship, Sir," I said, giving Enah 2 (E2) what information we had at the time. "But it has no markings to tell us of its origin. And our sensors can't identify what the ship was made out of. There is also some miscellaneous space debris."

"Elaytay (Tay), make note of it in the logs," came Captain Enah 2 (E2)'s orders.

"Done, Sir!" I replied. So I made an entry in the ship's records of the size of the mass found and made note of the nature of the debris and its location.

"That was a close one," piped in Meninso's response as the color came back to his face.

"Not really; I had it under control all along," came Paleeto (Pal)'s retort in a loud voice.

"If that be so, then why all the dramatics?" Meninso questioned.

"Well, it seemed that everything was getting boring," Paleeto (Pal) said, with a slight smile.

"You just handle the navigation and let us be bored," Meninso's reply.

"Alright! That's quite enough of that. A bit of excitement never hurt anyone," Enah 2 (E2) interrupted.

Everything was quiet for a while after that except for the laughter of Elmosa (Mosa). Meninso had gone back to playing games with him. Everyone else went back to doing whatever it was they were doing before all of the excitement.

I went and sat down next to Paleeto (Pal).

"Was all that really just for show or could there have really been a problem?" I questioned in a low voice so that no one else could hear.

"Well, I guess that if I hadn't been taking care of my job correctly, there could have been some problems if we had run into the debris. It looks like that may have been what happened aboard the other ship if that's what it was. I mean there weren't any signs of foul play or attacks, so I figure their sensors didn't pick up the space debris we detected, or they would have gone around it. And so, yes, I decided to have some fun with it," Paleeto (Pal) said with a low voice and a smile.

"Well on my first mission we weren't so lucky. That's why you came on this mission to get me. Our ship sensors didn't pick up space debris or wreckage as quickly as the sensors do now and we hit some, lost the controls and crashed. So that hit home pretty hard for me," I said.

"I'm sorry. I wasn't told what had happened on your mission. I was just told to be the navigator and that we were coming to pick up a female person that had been stranded on Earth," Paleeto (Pal) explained.

"Oh, that's okay, but next time you decide to do something like that, give me a small smile, okay?" I requested.

"Sure, a small quick smile. Good Friends?" Paleeto (Pal) asked.

"Yes, by all means, good friends." I said, relieved.

Chapter Thirteen
DNA Experiments

"Well, all is clear, and we will be entering orbit in 12 keptrons (minutes) and 13 microns (seconds)," Paleeto (Pal) said with a smile as he looked over his shoulder at me.

I smiled back with excitement. I looked around the ship and everyone was busy doing things. Strong Bow and Elmosa (Mosa) were watching a holographic movie together. So I decided to go through some of the things we had brought back with us for gifts and keepsakes.

Time went whizzing by very quickly. "We are coming about for orbit," Paleeto (Pal) announced.

Good, I thought as I went to my post at communications. "We have made contact and receiving landing instructions now!" I announced.

"I have the heading correction, they are set and landing is a go," came Paleeto (Pal)'s voice loud and clear.

"Good team work people," Enah 2 (E2) said applauding us as we landed.

"Are we at our new home?" Elmosa (Mosa) asked as he jumped up and down next to me.

I looked up at Strong Bow who by this time was standing next to me. "Elmosa (Mosa) we are home." I answered with a smile as I placed my hand gently on his head to stop his jumping.

A few microns (seconds) later the ship door was opening, and just on the other side I could see my Gramps. "Gramps! Gramps!" I shouted with happiness as I got up and ran for the door, and by that time, Grams was standing beside him.

Our arms went around each other in the way I believe could have very well been the grandest hug this side of Cyterrious. When the hugging and the reunion had slowed down, I turned to Strong Bow and introduced him and Elmosa (Mosa) to them. They were given a very warm welcome.

As we were leaving the ship, Enah 2 (E2) reminded me that we had brought things back with us.

"Well, I guess I can have them sent over to your grandfather's home later," Enah 2 (E2) suggested.

"Oh, would you please Sir? It has been so long since I have been with Grams and Gramps," I requested as I looked back over my shoulder at Enah 2 (E2).

"Yes, this time. But, I will need your help with the DNA samples later, okay?" he remarked with an understanding smile.

"Yes, I will report later. Give me five decons (hours), okay?" I asked.

"See you then," Enah 2 (E2) said as he waved us on.

"Oh, by the way, I have your graduation papers at home. They sent them over after they found out you were alive. You are now an officer in the United Planets Alliance," Gramps proudly announced.

Once we were out of the ship and back on solid ground, Elmosa (Mosa) started with the questions. Most of them were for his grandparents. I was glad for that because it gave me a chance to notice all the changes that had taken place while I was gone. I happened to look over at Strong Bow while we were on our way back to Grams' house. He was sitting motionless in the transport with his mouth slightly agape and his eyes wide. I put my hand gently on his leg. He jumped with a start. Then he noticed it was just me.

"This is so different from our Earth home," he said as he started to speak slowly.

"Oh? Well, there are a lot of things that are different from Earth," I retorted.

When we got to Grams' house and walked up the front steps, we were bombarded by a wall of wonderful smells.

"Wha?," I started.

"Oh, Grams has been cooking the old way again," Gramps interrupted.

"Oh. Good eats this sestron (day)," I announced as I turned to Strong Bow and Elmosa (Mosa).

"We received word of your arrival about three pestrons (weeks) ago," announced Grams.

"I love you both so much," I said as I put my arms around them again and we all walked into the house.

The table was all set. "Sit down all of you," Grams said waving at us. So we all three sat down and Grams and Gramps both got busy carrying the food to the table.

"This is a celebration feast, yes?" asked Strong Bow.

"Yes, my son, it is a celebration of all you coming home to us. Now our family is greatly blessed. We have a grandson and a great grandson to add to the family. We are all very blessed with your safe arrival," said Gramps as he and Grams both sat down.

We all ate our fill and enjoyed each other's' company. Grams and Gramps had a chance to get to know Strong Bow and Elmosa (Mosa) a little better.

As we were visiting, I looked at my timelink. "Oh, no! If I don't hurry I'm going to be late meeting Enah 2 (E2). We have a lot of work to do before evening."

"You go right ahead, dear. We will take good care of our new grandson and great grandson," Gramps said with a smile while motioning for me to hurry.

I remember reaching over to give Strong Bow a hug before leaving but he stood up and embraced me lovingly and gave me a kiss. By that time Elmosa (Mosa) was standing beside us and was giving us both a hug. Strong Bow picked him up and I gave him a hug and a kiss. "Now you be good for Grams and Gramps while I'm at work."

"They will both be fine," Gramps interrupted. "I have things I want to show them."

At that, I waved and went running down the front steps. As I ran I kept track of the time on my timelink. If I hadn't run fast I would have been late.

I finally arrived at the research lab. Enah 2 (E2) was bent over a lagascope. "Ah, you're here, good, Come here and take a look at what I've found."

As I looked at what he had on the slide, I could see that in this sample of DNA, only half of it was salvageable. "So, what can we do with only half of a sample? Do we throw it out or try an experiment and see

what we end up with?" I asked, half of me
hoping the answer would be experiment.

"Well, it depends on how much time
you want to spend on the project," came back
the answer from Enah 2 (E2).

"Well since we have never had
anything like this to work with, why don't
we go to the Creation Domes on Palids?" I
said before Enah 2 (E2) interrupted.

"We don't have to go all the way to
Palids now. We have our own set of Creation
Domes," he advised me.

"Oh! That is great, really great. There
are so many things that can be learned in a
Creation Dome," I heard myself say
excitedly, almost without thinking. "Can we
use them now?"

"Okay, I can't think of any reason
why we can't feed all the information we
have on the chromosomes to the Creation
Dome's compulinks and see where it leads
us," Enah 2 (E2) finally answered after
thinking about it.

So we left the labs and headed for the
Creation Domes with all the information we
had. Our journey was short, only about 2

keptrons (minutes). After working on the sample for a while, we finally got a response. I can't say that it was the one we were looking for, but at least it was a response.

Enah 2 (E2) finally asked, "What did you say this DNA was from?"

I looked on my records, "It is supposed to be a rabbit." I said.

He looked puzzled.

"Oh, I'm sorry, a rabbit is a mammal about one and one half lifnas (feet) long when adult, and has long ears, big eyes, four feet, and a short tail. But I think that the DNA that governed its size got lost somewhere," I continued with a chuckle.

"I think you are right about that," he said, as we both stood there looking at what was the largest rabbit I believe I will ever see. I mean this rabbit was four lifnas (feet) long and when it stood on all fours, its head was almost three lifnas (feet) from the ground.

"I think we had better leave this DNA sample alone and not do it for real," I said, and Enah 2 (E2) nodded his head in agreement. "I am glad that rabbit was only a holographic rabbit. Can you imagine what life would be like with a herd of that size rabbit running around?

So we both decided to destroy that sample of DNA. After all, that was only one sample out of close to 50. So we went back to the lab and started work on more of the samples. We worked in the lab till it was real late and our work was interrupted by a call from Gramps, saying it was time to quit for the night. So when we got to a stopping point, I said goodnight to Enah 2 (E2) and left.

Chapter   Fourteen
Watapaw

By the time I arrived back at Gramps' house, an excited Elmosa (Mosa) was waiting for me at the door, dancing around. As I walked into the house, I picked him up and asked him why he was still up. He was so excited that all of his speech was garbled. I gave him a hug and a kiss and put him down, And looked over at Gramps. "Okay, what have you two been up to while I've been at work?" I asked Gramps with a smile.

"Oh, a little of this and a little of that," was all the answer that he gave me.

I remember looking at Strong Bow who was sitting contently in a large chair in the corner. Then he gave me this large smile, got up, gave me a kiss and told me, "We have had a good sestron (day). There are lots of things to see and do here."

"Now, I'm going to get an answer to my question some time tonight," I said as I started to laugh. "You guys might as well let me in on your secret. Now what happened that made Elmosa (Mosa) so excited?"

Strong Bow looked at Gramps and they both started to laugh. Elmosa (Mosa) by that time was in front of them jumping up and down saying, "He's mine, all mine."

I stooped over to talk to Elmosa (Mosa). "What is it that is all yours?" I asked him while glancing back up at Gramps and Strong Bow.

"A watapaw, a watapaw, that's what, and he's all mine," Elmosa (Mosa) blurted out.

Gramps started to laugh, "I guess the opawtar is out of the bag." He said looked at Strong Bow.

"Yeah, it looks like the rabbit got away," Strong Bow replied.

"Now this isn't fair at all. Just what is a watapaw?" I asked. "Before I left for the Earth mission there wasn't anything called a watapaw on this planet. So will someone fill me in as to what a watapaw is, please?" I asked with my curiosity aroused.

"Yes, I know that when you left to go on your mission things were much different than now. We now have our own Creation Domes. We have new and strange animals and people from other planets living and working in exchange for some of our own people. The other planets send some of their people here to learn our ways and show us their inventions and we send some of our people to their planet to do the same. We have found by doing this we all learn much more and there are fewer misunderstandings. But getting back to the fun at hand, a watapaw is an animal that came from Odock 4, the planet in the next solar system. It stands almost my height at its back. It walks on all fours."

Then Strong Bow interrupted. "It looks almost like one of our earth horses, except for its head and tail."

Then he was interrupted by Gramps with a laugh, "This is my story, okay?"

"You are right, Grandfather. Go on," Strong Bow relinquished the conversation.

"Well as Strong Bow was saying, it looks like the earth horse except for his head," Gramps looked at Strong Bow and they both laughed.

"Okay, except for its head, and….?" I prodded.

"Okay," Gramps started, and then Elmosa (Mosa) jumped in.

"Just come and look," he grabbed me by the hand, "Come look!" and almost dragged me out the door to the back yard.

"Gramps received word before you landed that we had a great grandson and he prepared a surprise for him," said Grams as I went through the back door.

'There standing very peacefully in front of me was what I would have had to agree was the strangest sort of animal I had ever seen. The body was the size of a horse, but it was shaped sort of like a large cat with' paws that had longer digits than a cat, almost like fingers and it had a long prehensile tail like a monkey. The head however was another story and hard to believe. It had large, almost floppy ears and a long mane like the

Earth lion that I could remember seeing pictures of when I was younger. It had large beautiful dark eyes, a short nose, but not flat, and the mouth of this animal was that of a grazer.
"Strange, strange indeed.' I thought to myself

"When I got word that you were on your way home, I made sure that there would be plenty of things to do and learn for my great grandson. So I put this area together and bought a watapaw. They are very quiet animals and they love people. They are really good with children. On their home planet they are known as the children's playmates," Gramps said.

By that time, Elmosa (Mosa) had climbed up the fence and onto the back of the watapaw. "See, Mom? See? He likes me!" Elmosa (Mosa) said with joyous laughter.

So we stood and watched Elmosa (Mosa) ride around in circles on the back of the watapaw.

"What if the animal was to start running and Elmosa (Mosa) was to get hurt?" I questioned Gramps.

"Oh, that will never happen. The watapaws are very intuitive animals; they can read the thoughts of a young child. That is why you get a watapaw when the child is very young, so they can get to know the child as they grow older. Don't worry. Elmosa (Mosa) will be just fine. He is a very smart boy," came the answer with little comfort from Gramps.

"Well, I don't know. It looks very strange and I don't know anything about it," I remarked.

"Not to worry. Grams and I studied everything we could get our hands on about the watapaw. And you know how thorough your Grams is," Gramps explained.

"Well in that case I guess it will be okay," I remarked with a grin at Gramps. "Not to mean that you aren't thorough in your studies," I added.

Gramps laughed, "I knew what you meant. Don't worry so much or you may turn into a worrywart. I've heard that they aren't too pretty."

"Uck! What a thought," Strong Bow chimed in.

"Okay! Okay, I'll lighten up. It takes time to get used to all the changes here now. I mean everything seems so different," I said with a laugh.

"Yes, there have been quite a few things changed since you were here last," Gramps added.

"Hey all of you noise makers, it's getting late. I know we have lights out there but we all need our rest, especially little ones. After all, we all want him to grow big and strong," came a voice out of the dark. Then the back porch light came on and we could see that it was Grams with her head stuck out the back door.

"Okay, okay, love, we're coming," Gramps yelled to Grams and then turned to us. "Well you all heard. Oh, my! It is a lot later than I thought," he added as he looked down at his timelink.

"Okay, Kiddo. It's time to get off the watapaw and let it rest, too," I said as I reached out for Elmosa (Mosa).

The watapaw heard what I said and brought Elmosa (Mosa) to an area on the fence where he could climb off easily.

As I carried Elmosa (Mosa) to the house, I asked, "Elmosa (Mosa), what are you going to call your new friend?"

"I don't know yet, I have to dream on it, okay?" came his answer. I was almost taken back by his answer. I may have expected an answer like that from an older child, but he seemed so young.

"Yes, that's fine. When you find its name then you can tell me, okay?" I answered after a few microns (seconds).

We all continued into the house and said our good nights and went to sleep.

Chapter Fifteen
Kerzna (Kerz)

Bright and early the next morning, we, (Grams, Gramps, Strong Bow, and I) were all sitting in the kitchen having some tea, warm bread and visiting while waiting on the rest of breakfast to finish cooking. All of a sudden we could hear a loud thump, two slams and the thudding of Elmosa (Mosa)'s moccasins as he ran down the stairs, through the hallway and toward the kitchen. Gramps stood at the kitchen door ready to grab him as he ran through.

"Gotcha! Now where are you going so fast?" Gramps howled, with laugher as he swung Elmosa (Mosa) over his shoulder and then put him down.

Elmosa (Mosa) was laughing excitedly, too. You could see the excitement on his face.

"Mama I know his name!" Elmosa (Mosa) announced while hopping on one foot, then the other.

"Wait, whose name? Slow down just a keptron (minute) and tell me what you are talking about," I requested.

"The watapaw, Mama, the watapaw's name," he shouted with excitement, while jumping up and down.

"Oh! Well tell us what his name is, quick, before you go through the floor," chimed Grams with a chuckle.

Elmosa (Mosa) stopped jumping, stood very straight and tall and said, "Kerzna (Kerz)," with his hands on his hips.

"Kerzna (Kerz)? humm, Kerzna (Kerz)! Now that sounds like a really good name; a good name indeed!" rang out Gramps.

"Yes, a fitting name. Yes, real good, son," agreed Strong Bow.

Grams and I both nodded our heads at almost the same time.

"Yes, that is a nice name, love," I said as I gave him a hug.

Elmosa (Mosa) started for the door again, but on the way, he had to go past Grams. Now Grams had raised me most of my life and was plenty used to little ones wanting to go out to play before breakfast. In a flash, out went Grams' arm, scooping Elmosa (Mosa) up into the air, and she stood there holding him in her arms.

"Not so fast there, you! You have to eat something before you go outside. You will need all the energy you can get if you are going out to play with Kerzna (Kerz) this sestron (day)," explained Grams with a loving smile.

"Okay, Grams," came the reply as Elmosa (Mosa) shuffled slowly back over to the table and sat down.

"Why the long face? It won't take long for Grams to get you something to eat. She's pretty fast, too, you know?" Gramps said, patting Elmosa (Mosa) on the back.

Elmosa (Mosa) looked up and smiled. Grams was pretty fast in food preparation.

All of us had things to do. This sestron (day) promised to be very busy.

I had to help run more tests on the DNA samples I had gathered and others that had come in since. Gramps was going to show Strong Bow the Creation Domes and Grams and Elmosa (Mosa) were going to do fun things around the house and take a walk along the shoreline of the lake while letting Elmosa (Mosa) ride Kerzna (Kerz).

Grams knew all of the great place near the house to have lots of fun. She took Elmosa (Mosa) to a part of the lake where the white sand lay near the edge. This is where they found out that Kerzna (Kerz) could dig great holes and leave tall piles of sand.

It would soon be lunch time and they would need to head back home. Grams told Kerzna (Kerz) to try and get the sand and dirt off himself. Kerzna (Kerz) lumbered in disappointment down to the water's edge and put his great paws in the water, got himself a drink and stood there looking at the water. Elmosa (Mosa) ran down to help get the sand off his fur and they both got to playing in the water. Splashing and laughing and making some very strange noises and soon Grams got to laughing and playing with them till they all were wet.

The sun was shining brightly, so their clothes dried while she and Elmosa (Mosa) picked flowers and Kerzna (Kerz) rolled in the long grass on the way home.

When they got home it didn't take long for Grams to get lunch fixed. Elmosa (Mosa) ate fast so he could go play in the yard with Kerzna (Kerz).

Grams cleaned up and kept an ear on Elmosa (Mosa)'s laughter. Soon there was no sound and she stopped to go see what was going on. Grams knew like most moms that when children get quiet, it is time to check on them.

When she got to the front door she could see than Kerzna (Kerz) was lying out on the grass and Elmosa (Mosa) had fallen asleep between his large front paws with his head resting on Kerzna (Kerz)'s chest. Kerzna (Kerz) looked up at her and gave her a nod, letting her know that everything was good. With an easy breath she went back into the house to finish her work.

Kerzna (Kerz) was working out to be
a great friend and sitter for Elmosa (Mosa).

Chapter Sixteen
Mozla (Mol)'s Rescue

Many sectos (years) had passed and Strong Bow and Elmosa (Mosa) spend a lot of their time in the Creation Domes. Strong Bow became a teacher of survival on other planets. He held most of his classes in the Creation Domes.

Strong Bow had taken Elmosa (Mosa) to the Creation Domes a number of times with his two best friends, Mozla (Mol) and Rogna (Roger). Each time he took them to the Creation Domes, he would have the computers create a place that looked just like Earth and the tribal members. What he hadn't told Elmosa (Mosa) and his friends was that he had made the program of Earth, with the information he knew from his own people and their

ways of life. The Earth Program consisted
of Strong Bow's tribe, the way the land
looked, the same plants and animals that he
had grown up with and the personalities of
the people, even the children as they grew
up.

Well, Mozla (Mol), Rogna (Roger),
and Elmosa (Mosa) liked what they saw and
enjoyed camping there. Strong Bow had to
watch closely that the three boys didn't fall
in love with the girls in the program.

Mozla (Mol) and Rogna (Roger) was
an odd pair. They were both rather tall and
thin. Mozla (Mol) had almost black
shoulder-length hair and large blue eyes.
While Rogna (Roger) on the other hand was
a little shorter his hair was dark brown and
he had big green eyes.

All three of the boys all got along real
well and I always thought that one of the
main reasons was because all three of them
were of mixed peoples and planets. The boys
were lucky to have each other for friends.
The idea of intermarriages between people of
different planets was new, and with all new

ideas come teasing, prejudices and hurtful childish games.

The boys, Elmosa (Mosa) included, were all fun loving and of a gentle nature. They all enjoyed having fun and taking chances, but not the type of chances that were foolish and dangerous, so I never worried about them when they were together. I felt I was lucky. The boys were a good influence on each other.

Elmosa (Mosa) and his friends were old enough to go on camping trips of their own now. They loved new adventure and sometimes we all went camping together. The wilderness around our house was a nice place and of course, Kerzna (Kerz) was always with them. Kerzna (Kerz) seemed to like going camping with the boys. One late afternoon, Rogna (Roger) came running up to the house--panting and out of breath.

"Strong Bow!" Came a winded yell from outside. Strong Bow and Gramps put down the project they were working on and went to the door where they saw Rogna (Roger) darting towards the house.

"Rogna (Roger), what's the matter?" Strong Bow asked.

Rogna (Roger) had a chance to catch his breath a little better by now. "Mozla (Mol) and, well, we were camping up by Mossca Flats and, well,"

"Just tell us what's wrong!" interrupted Gramps.

"Come on, I'll tell you on the way, but," Rogna (Roger) held up his hand to stop Strong Bow, "better get the rope. We may need it," he continued.

Strong Bow grabbed the rope that hung on the side of the storage building on his way out of the yard.

"Now tell us what happened," Strong Bow said.

"Well, everything was going really good until we got to talking about girls, and Mozla (Mol) said he liked Morning Star in the Earth program that you made for all of us. And Elmosa (Mosa) and I tried to tell him that Morning Star wasn't a real person and he got mad and stomped off. I guess he wasn't paying attention to what he was doing and he got too close to the edge of the cliff and the

rocks gave way. Anyway, he's on the ledge
below camp, about 10 lifnas (feet) down. He
doesn't seem to be hurt badly," Rogna
(Roger) explained.

When Strong Bow, Gramps and Rogna
(Roger) got to the camp, they found that
Kerzna (Kerz) had saved Mozla (Mol) and
that everyone was okay. Everyone gave
Kerzna (Kerz) lots of hugs and pats and
packed up the camping gear and headed for
the house.

I had just come home a few microns
(seconds) after the guys had left on the
rescue. Grams filled me in on what was
happening from what she had overheard
Rogna (Roger) telling Gramps and Strong
Bow.

I could see them coming up the path
towards the house. Grams and I went and
waited at the gate for them.

"Good. I see that everyone is okay. So
someone tell us what happened," I said and
Grams nodded from behind me.

"When we got there everything had
been taken care of," said Gramps.

"When I left Elmosa (Mosa), Mozla (Mol) and Kerzna (Kerz), Mozla (Mol) had just fallen over the cliff to a ledge below. I knew he wasn't hurt really bad so I came for help," Rogna (Roger) said.

"It all started because of girls!" Mozla (Mol) said.

"Girls?" I asked.

"Yeah, girls! We were talking about who we liked and Elmosa (Mosa) said that Elnona (Nomie) was cute and he liked the way she talks." I turned and looked at Elmosa (Mosa) and smiled. He looked at me and turned red. Strong Bow reached over and put his arm around Elmosa (Mosa) and whispered something in his ear. "Rogna (Roger) said he didn't have a girlfriend and I said I like Morning Star. That's when all the ruckus started. They were both telling me that Morning Star isn't real. I know that, but I can still like her, can't I?" asked Mozla (Mol).

"Sure, you can like anyone you want, but you must realize that you can't have a real life with a person created in the Creation Domes, okay?" Strong Bow explained.

"Sure, I know that. But I wasn't planning a life with Morning Star! But I would just like to find someone like her," Mozla (Mol) said.

"Well, now that may be possible. But that's nothing to get in a fight over, right?" I said as we walked to the house. Grams had already gone in to prepare dinner and I couldn't help but wonder if this Morning Star was the same Morning Star that I knew on Earth as Strong Bow's little sister. I made a mental note to ask Strong Bow about this when the boys weren't around to overhear us.

"Okay," came the answer from all three of the boys.

"Now, will someone tell Grams and me how Mozla (Mol) got up from the ledge?" I asked.

Elmosa (Mosa) started the story. "Well, as you know, Mozla (Mol) fell over the side of the cliff. Kerzna (Kerz) is the real hero. He pushed over this small tree and handed it down to Mozla (Mol) with his tail. Mozla (Mol) put it against the side of the cliff and climbed up as far as he could. He tried to reach for my hand, but I couldn't reach him. So Kerzna (Kerz) put his claws into another tree that was near the edge. I was laying on the edge talking to Mozla (Mol) when Kerzna (Kerz) wrapped his tail around my knees. I knew he wouldn't let me fall, so I went over the edge and reached for Mozla (Mol). When we had a good hold on each other... Kerzna (Kerz) pulled us both back up to the top of the ledge, and we were all safe. The End."

"Kerzna (Kerz) is a hero," Mozla (Mol) interrupted.

By that time Grams had made something for all of us to eat. We all sat on the porch and ate our meal and stroked Kerzna (Kerz) while he ate his favorite fruit. Grams had made a special meal for him, too.

"Kerzna (Kerz) is the best animal friend a boy could have," I said as I smiled at Kerzna (Kerz). I could almost say I saw him smile back at me.

Chapter Seventeen
Ready to Go Again

A few mistrons (months) have passed, and then one night I got home before Strong Bow and Elmosa (Mosa). Giving me a chance to talk to Gramps a few keptrons (minutes) alone. "I feel a need to go back to Earth and help our other families with some of their medical problems and I've talked to the council already and have received their permission."

"Well, if you think this is what you really need to do, and you already have permission, there isn't too much left for me to say." he said looking back over his shoulder at Grams.

She was smiling and nodding her approval.

"Then" Gramps started to say something else, but...

Hearing the front door open, I didn't get a chance to hear Gramps thoughts. Strong Bow and Elmosa (Mosa) walked in the door and right behind them were Mozla (Mol) and Rogna (Roger). These two stayed at our house while their parents were out on missions, which was pretty often.

"Strong Bow, I need to talk to you, please?" I said, heading him off from the kitchen..

"Excuse me boys, I will be right back," he said, excusing himself with a slight bow.

"Hello, love. What do you want to see me about?" he questioned as he greeted me with a hug.

"Well, how would you like to go back to Earth to see our families again; just for a short visit? Nothing really long, maybe just for a few pestrons (weeks) or so?" I asked.

"You mean it? Do you mean really and truly go back to Earth for a real visit? You mean it for real?" he asked excitedly, like a small child on Laufenos (Christmas).

"Yes, love, I mean for a real visit. But we will also be doing work there, too. You do understand that part, too, don't you?" I said looking for a quick answer.

"Yes, dear, I know by now that if the council approves anything that there has to be another reason for it, too. But I do, really do want to go to Earth again. I miss my parents and little sister, Morning Star. But what about Elmosa (Mosa)? And how many people can come on this mission? And what other reason will the council have?" Strong Bow asked concerned about the answers.

"We can take as many as five with us, besides the normal ship's crew," I answered. Then I remembered I wanted to ask him about Morning Star in the Creation Domes' Earth Program. "A thought just came to me. Is this Morning Star in the program you run, your little sister, but older than when you left?" I asked.

"Uh, yeah," Strong Bow said slowly with a shy smile. "Close but not exact, because the only information I could give the program was the rules I knew she would be raised by and her personality I knew when I left. And you know as well as I do that other things may have happened to make her different," he explained. "Why"

"Just thinking of some of the complications and explaining you may have to do," I retorted.

"When Mozla (Mol) meets the real Morning Star, boy, what a mess this could be," I thought to myself.

"Can I tell the boys now?" he asked interrupting my thoughts.

"Yes, I had a feeling that you would want to take Elmosa (Mosa)'s best friends, that's why I asked the council for permission to bring five people. But the boys have to complete a lot of their training in only three pestrons (weeks)," I answered.

"Good. So we leave in just three pestrons (weeks). I think they can do it. They're smart and learn quickly," Strong Bow said with a nod as he left the room. I could hear, in the other room, the shouts of happiness and laughter ringing out as Strong Bow told the boys about the trip.

I contacted Mozla (Mol) and Rogna (Roger)'s parents and received their permission for the boys to go with us.

The boys now ranged between the ages of 13 and 15 sectos (years). Rogna (Roger) and Mozla (Mol) were older than Elmosa (Mosa) by a secto (year) and one half and two sectos (years). Because Rogna (Roger) and Mozla (Mol) were taking accelerated courses, they were ready to graduate from the Academy, so the council was going to let them use this trip as their first mission.

Elmosa (Mosa) would be allowed to go because we were his parents and it was our mission.

The boys all studied hard and fast to finish their studies before we were to leave. They were so excited, the trip is all they talked about for the rest of the pestron (week).

Sestrons (days) went by quickly and I was given a tour of the new ship we were taking on this trip. I was surprised to find that all of the equipment had been improved. Now in an emergency, the new science scout

ships could be handled by only two crewmembers.

Chapter Eighteen
New Crew

The pestrons (weeks) passed quickly and we were all packed and ready to leave. We were taking medical supplies, medicines, herb seeds and seedlings with us as part of our mission. While we were there, we would be giving the whole tribe physical examinations.

There was only a few sestrons (days) left before we were to leave on the Earth mission when I finally got a chance to glance at the crew list; it was lying on the computer desk in the lab. I found that Paleeto (Pal) was going to be our navigator, and that I was serving as science and communications officer again. The captain was a newcomer to our planet. His name was Norzalon (Red). His hair is red, and he has dark eyes, (said the description out by his name). Now that was a strange combination, I was used to red hair with green or blue eyes and dark skin.

I was sitting at one of the compulink and recording DNA data from the tests taken that sestron (day), when I was interrupted.

"Hello!" came a voice I didn't recognize. I looked up, and there stood a man who was short and stocky with red hair. His bushy beard was darker than the hair on his head. He had very light skin in contrast to his very dark eyes and very dark beard. I thought to myself that this man must be our captain named on the mission's crew list.

I smiled and said, "Hello," returning the greeting.

"I am called Norzalon (Red). I am assigned to be the captain on the Earth Mission. I was told you would be here in the lab. You are Lieutenant Elaytay (Tay), yes?" he inquired.

"Yes, Sir," I said as I stood to greet him properly. We shook hands and I made a shallow bow in respect.

"I know this planet Earth. My people have been to it before and, in fact, some of them are still there. My people have a village in the northern sector of the largest land mass near the snow country," he said.

What he said sort of took me by surprise. "I didn't know that any of the planets in the Alliance had colonies on the Earth," I said.

"Oh, we put up the village before we joined the United Planets Alliance, and they didn't make us take our people off the planet, so we stayed," he explained.

"So what do you call this village?" I asked.

"It is called Norz-men. It was my great grandfather who helped settle the village and so it was named after him," he said.

"How long have your people been exploring space?" I asked.

"I'm not really sure, but I know that it has been a long time. I was born on the planet known as Kortona. It's in the third solar system. But I have called many planets home since I have served the United Planets

Alliance. You see, our people have a long life span. I am now 215 Earth years," he said.

"Well then you must have seen a lot of things I've only dreamed of through-out the universe," I speculated.

"Well, maybe so. I've lived on 12 planets besides my own, counting this one and visited nine more in science explorations. I plan to see and do a whole lot more before I stop serving with United Planet Alliance." he said as he straightened proudly. "Well, I have work I must finish before we leave. But I did want to take the time to meet all of my crew before we got on the ship. I will see you later. Bye, Bye," he said as he waved and walked out the door.

I, too, had a few things I must get finished before leaving on this mission. I looked back at the compulink screen to refresh myself as to where I was on the test results and entering the data. To my surprise, I found I would be through in about ten keptrons (minutes). Then time was mine for a while.

On my way back home to Grams' house, I came across Paleeto (Pal) sitting under the boonak tree reading.

"Paleeto (Pal)," I said using telepathy. Paleeto (Pal) looked up with a big grin on his face. "Ah, you remember how," he said.

"Of course I do! I don't forget very easy and you, of all people, should know that," I retorted.

"Yes, I will be going on the Earth trip with you; it will give me a chance to see and talk to Healing Waters again. I like her. She is funny and I think that your papa, Two Wolves, will get the hang of talking by telepathy like me very soon. Plus, being on Earth again will give me a little bit of time to explore the countryside. Oh, yes, before I forget: I have been giving Elmosa (Mosa), Rogna (Roger) and Mozla (Mol) some exercises so they can develop their telepathic gift. I didn't think you would mind," Paleeto (Pal) said.

"No, I don't mind if you help the boys develop their gift. I will see you soon, I need to get home to my family." I said as I turned to walk home.

"Wait!" he said waving one hand, "Are all three of the boys coming on the mission with us?" he asked.

"Yes, they are, the mission papers said we have room for five plus the regular crew and I thought it might be educational for them," I said as I smiled, waved good-bye and left.

As I neared home, I could see the boys outside by one of the larger trees. As I got even closer, I saw they were playing with a few of the Earth animals we had cloned from the DNA samples I collected on my last trip to Earth.

"Hi, boys. What are you doing?" I asked.

"Oh, just playing around with some of the animals of Earth," answered Mozla (Mol).

"Hi, Mom," Elmosa (Mosa) said as he gave me a hug. "We've been learning how to get the animals to do what we ask through telepathy, just like Paleeto (Pal) said," he added.

"Well I guess that's okay, but remember that there are proper times to use this gift on animals? And you don't force any living thing to do something against its will except maybe in a real emergency. I mean life or death," I said.

"Yes, of course. Paleeto (Pal) has explained all that to us, and he also said that we must have the permission of the animal before we ask them to do anything. He also said there are times of importance, like danger to people when we can command animals in a different way to protect others even without the permission of that animal. But we must be careful how and when we use our gift," Elmosa (Mosa) explained, while the other two boys nodded their heads.

"Okay, carry on. It seems that Paleeto (Pal) has given you the ground rules for this gift. I'll see you later," I said as I walked towards the house.

"Oh! Hello dear. Did you know that the boys are using telepathy?" Grams asked meeting me at the door.

"Yes, and they seem to have the rules down pretty well," I said.

"I am so proud of them. I wasn't sure if they had any of the gifts or not. I mean, you know, with them being of interplanetary mixed backgrounds, I was afraid that the gifts may have skipped them," Grams commented.

"Yes, I know what you mean. I was wondering, myself, if the gifts would start to show, and if so, how long it was going to take. Oh! While we are on the subject of gifts, do you think that Gramps would mind teaching the boys a few more things, since he was the one who taught me?" I asked.

"I don't see why he wouldn't want to. He seemed to enjoy teaching you. Why not ask him yourself? He should be home soon," Grams said.

I sat down in Gramps's favorite chair near the window to read and watch the boys. I had only read a few pages when I looked up and spotted Gramps walking up to the boys.

I put down my book and watched. Gramps seemed to know exactly what the boys were doing. He stood and talked to them for a while, then all the boys nodded and Gramps continued towards the house.

I met Gramps at the door. "Hi, Gramps," I said while giving him a big hug.

"Hi, little darling. So how did your sestron (day) go?" he asked as we came into the house.

"Just great, real good. When I got home I found that Paleeto (Pal) had taught the boys how to use telepathy," I said.

"Yes, so I found out just now," he said giving me a strange look.

"What's with this look?" I asked.

"Well, sometimes when people like Paleeto (Pal), who are born with the gift of telepathy fully developed, teaches telepathy to others, they leave out some important exercises; little things that would make it easier to use for people who are normally non-telepathic. They don't teach these exercises because they don't have to develop those steps for the process," he said.

"So did you teach the boys those exercises while you were outside with them?" I asked.

"Yes, I did. I told them the same things I told you when you were first learning to use the power of telepathy. To practice with cards of different colors and with different symbols on them, like the square, circle, triangle, simple pictures and the like," he said.

"Good, I'm glad, Gramps. Would you mind teaching the boys some of the exercises that will help them to activate other gifts, such as levitation, teleportation, disappearing, walking through third-dimensional matter, and others that will lead them a little farther along the power path before we have to leave on the Earth mission?" I asked.

Chapter Nineteen
Learning Telepathy

"No, I wouldn't mind at all. In fact, I would gain great pleasure from it," he said. "But you know, I'll only have time to give them the basics before you have to leave in three sestrons (days). That means that you will need to give them the finer points," he added.

"Yes, I understand; that's no problem. It's just that right now I don't have enough time to teach them and get the last things ready for the mission, too," I said.

"I understand and, yes, I will be more than glad to help," he said putting his arm around me and giving me a hug. "But there is only so much I can teach them," he said. Then he turned to Grams who had just entered the room.

"Hello, love," she said with a kiss and a hug. "How did your sestron (day) go?" she asked handing him a warm cup of tea.

As they began their conversation, I smiled at both of them excusing myself. I went out on the front porch to swing and waited for the arrival of Strong Bow.

While I sat there on the porch, my mind wandered back to the stories I had heard, when I was younger. One stood out to me, it was about one point in our planet's history, when only the Holy Men were allowed to use the powers we all commonly use now. But even now we are taught that the powers are to be used only with great care and respect. The first and most important rule in using the powers is not to abuse the powers by using them for our own selfish gain or in a way that will harm anything in nature. Grams had always said, "Never use the powers to gain wealth or pleasure by forcing anyone or anything to do your bidding. Doing that would be like trying to place yourself above the Creator and it would be dangerous." I think these were the finer points that Gramps wanted me to teach the boys. As with anything you get, there are rules on what to do and what not to do with it.

Strong Bow was suddenly beside me and he bent over and kissed me.

"Oh, you're sneaky," I said in surprise.

"Not really," he laughed, "you were just deep in thought," he said as he sat down beside me and put his arm around me. "What happened to put you into such deep thought?" he asked.

"Did the boys talk to you on your way through the yard?" I asked looking out into the yard where the boys had been, but they were gone.

"No, I haven't seen them since I came home. Why? What's happened?" he asked.

"Well, Elmosa (Mosa), Mozla (Mol) and Rogna (Roger) have been learning the art of telepathy," I said.

"What is this tel-e-pathy?" he asked.

"Uh. Well, you remember Paleeto (Pal) on the rescue ship?" I asked.

"Yeah, the one that didn't like talking out loud and used his mind to talk instead?" he said.

"Yes, well, that kind of communication is called telepathy," I said.

"Oh, well, that's good isn't it? I mean that way you can talk to Elmosa (Mosa) wherever he is, right?" he asked.

"Yes. I guess that's true. I never thought of it in quite that way, but that's right," I said as I settled back to enjoy Strong Bow's company.

Grams came out onto the porch a few microns (seconds) later. "It's time to call the boys for dinner," she said.

"Okay, Grams," I said as she walked back into the house.

Strong Bow looked over at me and smiled. "You know, I think it's time to see how much they're learning," he said.

"What do you mean?" I asked.

"Well, use telepathy to call the boys to dinner," he said.

So I used telepathy to let the boys know it was time to eat. It wasn't but just a few keptrons (minutes) before all three of them came running around the corner of the house.

"What are we having?" asked the boys all at the same time.

Strong Bow and I looked at each other and smiled.

"I'm not sure. Grams just said to call you for dinner," I said.

We all went in and got ready to eat.

"I didn't hear you call the boys, Elaytay (Tay)," said Grams.

"That is because I didn't call them out loud. Strong Bow suggested checking on how far the boys had developed the power of telepathy. So I used it to call them to dinner," I said.

"It worked. We all heard the call for dinner," said Elmosa (Mosa).

"Well, I'm glad you listened because I am very hungry. So let's all go in and eat," said Gramps.

"Me, too," said Mozla (Mol) as all three of the boys hurried past us to the table.

Grams had everything on the table and dinner was ready to be served.

Chapter Twenty
Intro to Levitation

"Elaytay (Tay), Grams and I are
thinking about giving the boys a little
something else to think about, if that is okay
with you," said Gramps.

"Sure Gramps, you know best," I said.

The rest of us went in and sat down at
the table. We were passing around the dishes
and helping ourselves to each of them as
they came to us. As the potatoes were passed
to Gramps from one direction, Grams passed
him the salad at the same time from the other
direction.

Gramps reached out, took both, then
he left the salad floating in mid-air while he
helped himself to the potatoes.

"Uh," Rogna (Roger) said as if stunned, his mouth open and eyes large, pointing at the salad bowl.

"Oh, a little something I've picked up through the sectos (years)," said Gramps with a mischievous smile on his face.

"Teach me how to do that, Gramps," said Elmosa (Mosa) in excitement.

"Me, too! Me, too!" Rogna (Roger) and Mozla (Mol) said at the same time.

"What's it called?" asked Elmosa (Mosa).

"Levitation," said Gramps.

"Can you show us how right after we eat," asked Elmosa (Mosa).

"Maybe a little, we will see," said Gramps.

It was great to see and hear the excitement in the conversation for the rest of the meal. It was satisfying to see the strong desire for learning. Grams looked at Gramps and me and gave us her look of a "job well done".

"Can anyone learn to do these things?" Strong Bow asked.

"Well, I'm not sure, that remains to be seen. Shall we find out after dinner?" Gramps asked.

"I'm sure that Strong Bow has a good chance of being able to learn the powers. After all, Healing Waters was able to talk to Paleeto (Pal) using telepathy," I said.

"That's right," Strong Bow said beaming with delight.

"Well! With that kind of information, I guess we must at least try," said Gramps with a big smile.

After everyone had finished eating, I helped Grams with the cleaning and Gramps took everyone else into the study. Grams reached over behind a stack of books and turned on the comlink. I hadn't noticed it before. I guess Grams could see the surprise on my face.

"Oh this?" She asked pointing to the comlink. "This is a little something Gramps put in a few sectos (years) back. He said this way I would know everything that was going everywhere, if I wanted to," she said. "I don't use it that often, but I thought it might be fun tonight. I'm surprised you haven't noticed it before."

So we listened as we cleaned and giggled together at some of the comments and questions we were able to hear.

"Gramps definitely has everyone's undivided attention. I do have to say that Gramps is one of the best teachers I know," I said.

During the teaching session, Gramps went over the rules for both telepathy and levitation. Meanwhile, he had Strong Bow practicing the beginning exercises for telepathy.

"It may help if you can learn to visualize your words hanging in the air in front of you and then tell them where you want them to go," Gramps said to Strong Bow.

"Oh, yes. Now I see them," said Strong Bow.

"Okay, now tell the words where to go," instructed Gramps.

Within the time it took Gramps to finish his sentence, I heard the message in my head: "I love you darling, are you through cleaning yet?" came through very strong to me from Strong Bow.

I guess I must have stopped cleaning and looked odd, because after I heard the message, I noticed that Grams was looking at me. From the look on her face, I knew she had heard Strong Bow's message, too.

Grams said, "Send a reply, or he will think he's failed."

I smiled, nodded to Grams and sent the reply: "I love you too, very much and yes we are finishing up. Would you like me to bring you something?"

"Yes, please, a glass of water," was the reply Strong Bow instantly sent back to me.

Grams looked at me in a very pleased manner. "It seems that the Earth people carry a little of the power," she said.

"Yes, and I'm glad. He asked for a glass of water," I said smiling.

"Well, here," Grams said handing me a glass of iced water.

I took the glass and walked into the study. "Here is the water you asked for," I said with a big smile while handing Strong Bow the glass.

"I did it! I really did it!" he shouted.

"Yes, I guess you did! Now we know you can talk to Elaytay (Tay), but can you talk to others? And this time not only see your words but see who you are sending them to, this way only that person receives the message," said Gramps.

"Well, I'll try," said Strong Bow.

He sat and stared out into space for a few microns (seconds). Then, hearing a noise at the window, we all turned to see that Kerzna (Kerz) stood looking straight at Strong Bow and was just chattering away. Then he stopped and tilted his large head, and closed his dark eyes in a slow blink. Strong Bow got up and went over to pet Kerzna (Kerz) through the open window.

"You're a good friend, Kerzna (Kerz)," Strong Bow told Kerzna (Kerz) out loud.

We were all looking at Strong Bow when he turned and looked at us. We all wanted to know what Kerzna (Kerz) said.

"Well?" I said putting out my hand in a questioning manner.

"He said he was glad we have learned to use telepathy and that now when he needed something he could just ask for it, instead of waiting and maybe getting it," Strong Bow announced with delight.

We all laughed and nodded at Kerzna (Kerz). I could have sworn I saw him smile before he left the window.

The next two sestrons (days) seemed like a dream; they passed so fast. It was time for us to leave on the Earth mission. We were just waiting for the right orbital opening.

Finally, it was time for lift-off. We all stood in front of the ship and said our good-byes. At last we entered the ship, strapped in and began our spaceward climb towards Earth.

Other Book
by
Lauresa Tomlinson

Chapter Books

Elaytay (Tay)'s Adventures in Space and Time
(part two) We Meet Again
(part three) Time and Time Again

The Turning Stone

My Interview With a Fairy.

Magic Under The Pear Tree

There's an Alien in My Cereal

Secretly Special – You May Be Special Too

Crazy Déjà vu

Crazy Déjà vu – Not Again

Picture Books

Munchie and Goldie – Most Unlikely Friends
Cats in Charge
Sleepy Time Baby Bear

Other Books

Expressive Tree People
Studies of Life – Poems, Sonnets, Thoughts
zjavanee@gmail.com

www.ingramcontent.com/pod-product-compliance
Lightning Source LLC
Chambersburg PA
CBHW070305120726
47910CB00007B/2372